Exactly What

'Eleven short stories that add up
Virtuosity of technique accomp
and depth of characterization . . . Hinshaw's impressively
accomplished debut puts him in [Tim Winton and Jennifer
Egan's] company' Peter Kemp, *Sunday Times*

'A poignant demonstration of the way the past is still
folded into the present' *Financial Times*

'Such an incredibly clever idea this, a set of interlinked
stories in which people who appear in one turn up
in another . . . compelling' *Daily Mail*

'This is a notable debut from a smart and capable author.
Sentence by sentence, Ben Hinshaw offers wit, sensitivity
and sharp observation. Then slowly the reader sees the
grand design – the intricate, braided storylines, sustained
with energy and relish' Hilary Mantel

'Ben Hinshaw renders ordinary human agonies with
extraordinary precision and emotional insight. He
specializes in the atmosphere of human interconnection,
in subtle revelations and indelible images' Max Porter

'A splendid debut. The stories are sharp, subtle, richly
coloured and the world they deliver delightfully
surprising. Read this book' Lynn Freed, author
of *The Romance of Elsewhere*

'The calm, clear and intelligent prose belies the tortured
emotional currents just below the surface. Sophisticated
and ambitious' Samantha Dunn, author of *Failing Paris*

'Full of precise moments of humanity. So finely observed,
funny and touching' Alex Hyde, author of *Violets*

'Terrific. I really enjoyed it' Andy Miller, author of
The Year of Reading Dangerously and co-host of *Backlisted*

Ben Hinshaw was born on the island of Guernsey and has also lived in London and Northern California. His writing has received an O. Henry Prize and appeared in *Granta*, *Harvard Review*, *The White Review* and elsewhere. This is his first book.

Exactly What You Mean

BEN HINSHAW

PENGUIN BOOKS

PENGUIN BOOKS

UK | USA | Canada | Ireland | Australia
India | New Zealand | South Africa

Penguin Books is part of the Penguin Random House group of companies
whose addresses can be found at global.penguinrandomhouse.com.

First published by Viking 2022
Published in Penguin Books 2023
001

The permissions on p. 216 constitute an extension of this copyright page

Typeset by Jouve (UK), Milton Keynes
Printed and bound in Great Britain by Clays Ltd, Elcograf S.p.A.

The authorized representative in the EEA is Penguin Random House Ireland,
Morrison Chambers, 32 Nassau Street, Dublin D02 YH68

A CIP catalogue record for this book is available from the British Library

ISBN: 978-0-241-52473-2

www.greenpenguin.co.uk

For my parents

Don't they stay behind us, the questions of our lives, like fallen branches obscuring our view? To clear them away, even to thin them out, hardly occurs to us. We walk on, leave them behind, and from a distance they are certainly visible, but indistinct, shadowy, and all the more puzzlingly intertwined.

—Walter Benjamin, *One-Way Street*

1. The Charges

My brief friendship with Jacob Lovelong owed its existence to a lack of better offers. Still, for a while there, we were mates. I never really knew what he thought of me, or at least was never sure he thought much. But I like to believe he needed me back then just as much as I needed him.

He arrived after Easter break. It was 1994, my second year at Elizabeth College, and I was still passing lunch breaks alone in the library, or on a bench overlooking the tarmac tennis court. Lanky and big-eared as he was, with a walk like his knees were shackled, I instantly pegged him as a fellow outsider. At his first registration, instead of declaring 'home' or 'school' like the rest of us, he said 'present'. The room, already stifling giggles— that *name*—exploded. Jacob didn't flinch. When the housemaster explained that each boy must state his lunch plans, Jacob shrugged and said, 'I'll see how I feel.'

'In case of fire, Lovelong,' the housemaster shouted over the jeers, 'I'm afraid you must commit.'

Everyone went quiet. 'Home, I should imagine,' Jacob said. 'There's leftover salmon.'

That did it. I winced but also felt a surge of admiration. Didn't he know one slip could haunt you? Take, for example, the sixth-former who'd said, 'Here endeth the reading' (instead of 'Here ends') after delivering the Bible excerpt in assembly. Two terms on and boys of all ages were still adding -eth to verbs at will. 'You sucketh cock!' they cried as they passed. That salmon thing would follow Jacob for months, but he didn't seem to care.

One lunchtime that first week, he joined me on my bench. Didn't ask, just sat and crossed his legs and tucked into a wholemeal roll with ham, lettuce and tomato spilling out. (My own white-bread sandwich contained only Marmite and margarine.) I was reading Bernard Cornwell and crunching on cheese-and-onion Walkers. On the net-less tennis court, fifty boys chased a deflated football. Everyone had a centre parting, with curtains to the eyebrows—any longer and the VP would march you down to Mahy's for a trim. Jacob's hair, though, was a shapeless, curly mop, the colour of wet sand.

'Not going home today?' I eventually said.

He turned as if only just noticing me. 'Very perceptive. You must be a scholar.'

Which I was. Along with a dozen others in my year, my high 11-Plus score was sending me to Elizabeth at the taxpayers' expense. The rest, Jacob included, paid fees.

'If you must know,' he said, 'I'm preserving energy for swimming club later.'

'At Beau Sejour?'

'Bizarre name for a fucking leisure centre.'

The way he swore in a posh accent impressed me tremendously. What time, I asked, and when he said four, I told him that was my session too.

'My brother's in the squad,' I said. 'He swims five to six. Or "trains", I'm supposed to call it.' Ned was fifteen years old, Channel Islands champion in the 100m butterfly for his age. Sometimes he went to Jersey or the mainland to compete. My mother had decided that, rather than walk to the museum after school and wait for her to finish, I should swim twice a week too, then do homework in the café until she could pick us both up. Since I'd usually taken care of my homework at lunch, I was free to devote that post-pool hour to liquidating my pocket money, twenty pence at a time. 'You like arcade games?'

'What have they got?'

'*Wonder Boy. Out Run. 1942.*' I blanked. 'There's loads.'

'Those are all ancient. *Mortal Kombat?*'

I shook my head. 'They do get new stuff sometimes, though.'

A couple of boys from our year went by, hands in pockets, shirts untucked—tiny, pointless gestures of rebellion. 'Where's your salmon, Salmon?' one said. The other belched and laughed at the same time. Jacob ignored them. It was hardly affectionate, but I was still jealous that he already had a nickname.

'Want to walk over together later?' I said.

He shrugged. 'I need to get my trunks from home. But I suppose it's on the way.'

I offered him a crisp but he just wrinkled his nose.

That afternoon, once the last bell had rung, we walked back to his narrow, four-storey terraced house at the edge of Cambridge Park. At the green front door, he fished a key from his pocket. Even this seemed like a mainland affectation—our house was never locked.

'Wait here,' he whispered, leaving me on the steps out front. As he disappeared inside, I caught a glimpse of the hallway—hardwood floor, huge mirror, moody abstract painting of—trees? Trees or legs. When he came back out, he closed the door with extreme care, as if even the slightest disturbance might cause the house to collapse.

'Mum sleeping?' I said.

He passed me on his way down the steps. 'Dad, actually. And he's working, not sleeping.' His mother, he explained, worked at Deutsche Bank. Her job was the reason they'd moved from London.

In the changing room, surrounded by boys whipping welts on to one another with goggles or caps, I asked what his father did.

'Writing, mostly.' Jacob had an oddly protruding sternum, as if his ribcage had been squeezed from both sides at birth until the middle shifted tectonically out. 'Plays.'

A playwright moving from London to Guernsey? I pretended this made sense.

'Arcades after, then?' I said.

But he only turned and walked away, leaving me there as if we weren't both headed for the same lane full of spluttering, screw-kicking chumps.

He was good at some games, terrible at others. Once, he got so worked up playing *1942* that he kicked the machine and turned a toenail black. But ten minutes later, playing as Dhalsim, he reached a *Street Fighter II* level I'd never seen.

In June, a new game appeared. Or at least it was new to us—the machine itself had clearly been well used in its previous home. As we entered the gloomy arcade, I spotted it immediately. *Silver Sabre.* The graphics were magnificent, every pixel charged with life. The demo reel opened with a message from FBI Director William S. Sessions: *Winners don't use drugs.* Then a sinister figure appeared, tall, wide, stacked. A horned helmet-slash-mask revealed only his piercing eyes. His spiked shoulder pads seemed vaguely Chinese. This was Doom Viper, an evil renegade who had taken over the once peaceful kingdom of Zarna, and who now held the Zarnan king and his wife hostage in their castle. He had also stolen Zarna's sacred and magical emblem, the Silver Sabre.

Our mission was clear. Reach castle, slay Viper, reclaim sabre, free kingdom.

'The call is from destiny,' I said, part of a line from *The Simpsons.* Usually, one of us would set it up for the other to complete in their best Homer voice. But this time Jacob either didn't hear me or was too engrossed to speak.

He dropped twenty pence into the slot and we were introduced to his avatar, Lyra Flair. She had long brown hair, grey bikini, red knee-high boots, iron-grey sword. She reminded me of Flora, the older girl who'd lived next door for a while. Flora had liked to sunbathe in the garden and my mum had liked to complain about it. Where was Flora now, I wondered. As for Lyra Flair (Lyra Flora to me), having once rejected her royal upbringing, she was now, apparently, determined to redeem herself.

But, with Jacob at the controls, she was dead within thirty seconds, hacked down by a pair of grey-skinned ogres with spiked clubs. 'Bollocks,' he said, shoving in another coin. This time, beginning to learn the moves—jump-attack, twirl-and-stab—he got a bit further. From a sprite in a blue cowl he collected bottles of magic potion. These unleashed a fiery tornado, full of ghoulish faces, which wiped out a fair few bad guys. But pretty soon Jacob was out of change. With a nod, he stepped aside and I took his place. The joystick felt warm and clammy.

I got roughly as far as Jacob had before a mallet-wielding sumo clobbered my final life out of me. Reluctantly we stepped away to let some other kids try their luck. One was so young he could barely reach the controls.

My brother was already waiting outside with his mate Richard Sarre. Richard had recently become 'The Shark' by accepting a dare to swim up under a backstroking Alexis De Lisle and bite her on the bum. ('She loved it.') As usual, Ned and I ignored each other.

'That game is *quite* good,' I said to Jacob. That year, *quite* implied disdain for anyone who might fail to appreciate just how funny or big or crap something was. At school, I never said it for fear of being a try-hard. But with Jacob, I was safe.

'Relish,' he said, something he'd brought over from London. So far, it wasn't catching on.

When Mum pulled up, Ned got in the front—I didn't even try. I nodded to Jacob through the window of our Vauxhall Nova. He nodded back. It was agreed—for the final three weeks of term we would be skipping our hour in the pool altogether and devoting ourselves to Doom Viper's demise.

My brother had a job that summer—beach cleaning. Our father had helped him swing it, or so Dad claimed.

Every year, the States picked a dozen teens to spend their July and August mornings keeping the island's bays pristine. Eight till noon, six days a week. It only paid five quid an hour, but the work was unsupervised. Visits from States Works (two hungover middle-aged blokes in a yellow van, *Daily Sport* on the dash) were rare, if not mythical. Ned knew a guy who, the year before, hadn't picked up so much as a ring pull all summer, instead bringing full sacks from home and leaving them out for collection.

Ned got Soldiers' and Fermain. Both were close to home, though the path through Bluebell Wood that connected the two was hardly direct, and the cliffs meant a lot of steps. Still, he said, Fermain was sweet—no cars, no crowds.

On his first day, he got home at 12.15. I was eating beans on toast and waiting for *Neighbours* to come on. How was it, I asked.

'Tide was up so piece of piss. Fermain took about an hour. After that I just sat there with my Walkman.' *In Utero* had come out the year before and he was still playing it constantly.

Next day it rained and he was back before eleven. Not going to sit there getting soaked, he said. After that, he only ever did the full four hours when the sun was out.

Meanwhile I was spending more and more time with Jacob. My pocket money was five quid a week, and once a fortnight I would score another fiver by mowing my grandparents' lawn. I'd been saving hard for a Mega Drive, but now that was on hold. Most days, I would bike around to Jacob's, and he would leave a note telling his father that we'd gone to kick a ball or throw an Aerobie or 'shoot some hoops' in the park.

'The key to level five,' Jacob said one day as we crossed the playing fields, kicking our alibi ball ineptly between us, 'is saving enough magic for the pink knight.'

'So hard, though,' I said, punting the thing in his direction. 'Those skeletons with the shields are *quite* annoying.'

He swung a leg but missed, pale shins sticking out from baggy grey Mambo shorts. On top he had a bright red Quiksilver T-shirt—his mother bought him trendy clothes that lost their coolness the moment he put them on.

Near the skate park, I spotted Adam Beale and Gavin Chester. Two known rebels with broken voices, always in detention, hanging around with state-school girls. I knew their nicknames—Bubbles (an extension, I think, of Beale-zebub) and Cheese—but also knew I didn't have permission to use them. Both had undercuts, curtains hanging down over buzzed back-and-sides in a style forbidden at school. Both were smoking cigarettes, one arm around a girl. I tried not to stare as we passed, glancing up long enough to confirm that Jacob's T-shirt was—oh, shit—exactly the same as Beale's.

Chester noticed next, pointing and turning to laugh at Beale. The girls started creasing up too. I picked up the ball and widened my stride. Oblivious, Jacob was still banging on about the boss on level four.

Beale jumped up from the bench. 'Oi! Salmon Boy!' In a second, he was right in Jacob's face. 'Why you wearing my T-shirt, dickhead?'

Jacob turned away, screwing up his face, waving a hand under his nose. 'Polos? Mentos? Trebor Extra Strong? So many good minty options.'

Beale shoved him to the ground, kicked him in the gut and set about removing the T-shirt by force.

'Leave him,' I mumbled. I had to say something. But now Chester was on his feet too, and I had no interest in getting my head kicked in over an overpriced garment. The girls stayed on the bench, somehow looking both amused and bored by the spectacle.

Jacob was now face down and topless on the grass. His pale back was heavily freckled and moled. Beale was trying to rip the shirt in half. 'Where's that lighter?' he said. Chester produced a handsome Harley Davidson Zippo and smirked as Beale set the shirt on fire. It burned pretty well, and we all watched it disintegrate. The flames must have singed Beale's hand because he dropped it suddenly and tucked his fingers under his armpit. Jacob clambered up and stomped on the thing as if it might still be salvaged.

Beale smirked, though you could see the futility dawning on him. Now both shirts were ruined: one by fire, the other by association. He might as well have torched his own.

'That was illegal,' said Jacob shakily. 'Have fun in prison getting bummed senseless.'

He strode away. The prison remark had sounded funnier, I was sure, than he'd intended. Chester was in hysterics. Ball under arm, I caught up with Jacob. 'Thanks a fucking trillion,' he said. I mumbled an apology. I assumed we'd be heading back to the house, but half-naked Jacob made directly for the arcade. I don't know whether he was trying to save face or if he just really needed to play, but we managed about fifteen minutes before we got kicked out. 'It's not like there's a flipping heatwave,' the woman said. We took the long route back, avoiding the skate park. In brighter spirits, Jacob said that playing like that had actually been relish. Lyra, after all, only had her bikini.

I almost pointed out that he'd fallen through the gap in the bridge on level three, a move we'd long mastered. But I decided not to rip him when he'd finally cheered back up.

'Want a job?' my brother said. 'Half a job, anyway.' He was sick of cleaning Soldiers'. So many steps for so little rubbish. Did I want to take over? 'Fiver a day.'

I was squirrelling my way through a corn-on-the-cob, chin smeared with butter, watching *Home and Away*. 'That's half the work for quarter the pay.'

'It's not half.' Sweat patches bloomed from his pits and on his chest where his rucksack straps had been.

He'd recently started shaving and I could see the faint pixels of his stubble. 'Fermain is five times the size and gets ten times the rubbish, easily.'

Thirty quid a week on top of my pocket money and lawn-mowing cash. Unlimited *Silver Sabre*, plus extra to save for the Mega Drive. The downside was the early start. 'Does it have to be first thing?'

'Early doors, definitely.'

'But I thought –'

'Look, do it the way I tell you or don't bother. I'm sure The Shark or someone would –'

'Fine. I'll go at eight.'

Next morning, my alarm went off at 7.15. It was an overcast day, neither hot nor cold. I rode down the bumpy dirt path, ducking my head for low branches and brambles. At the top of the winding, overgrown steps hacked into the wooded cliff, I locked my bike to a low wire fence with ferns poking through. Being there alone was spooky, something I hadn't anticipated. I could see a few boats out on the open sea between Guernsey and Herm. The slick, metallic sea felt close and distant, everything echoing and muffled at once.

Sixty-eight steps. I pretended I was walking down to the stage in one of the Greek amphitheatres Mr Sheffrin had shown us in Classics, on one of the many occasions he'd delved into his personal slide collection. The tide was pretty high, the stony beach no bigger than a tennis court. I found a lone plastic bag, a few tiny polystyrene chunks. I could see why Ned had given up. No one was around to leave any litter or appreciate the lack of it. My black Casio said 8.25. I lay back on the egg-sized stones, wriggling to flatten them under my ribs, rucksack for a pillow. Seagulls drifted overhead, squawking. Apart from my brother, no one knew I was down there.

I was woken by footsteps on the stones. I sat up quickly, but the man I saw didn't look official. Mid-forties, black jeans and a matching T-shirt, dark hair parted neatly. His Hi-Tec Tennis trainers would have brought savage abuse on any kid unfortunate enough to wear a pair for PE. He carried an orange towel and a plastic bag striped white and blue. We were less than thirty metres apart, but he ignored me.

Head for the steps, I thought. But instead I sat there, looking out to sea, hoping the yellow gloves and sack beside me explained my presence.

I became aware that he was undressing. Fair enough, I thought, morning dip. But, as he hobbled into the water, I saw that he was naked. His arse cheeks were radioactively pale. He was skinny, with a gut. Edging in up to his bony thighs, he dived off the little ledge where the stones met flat sand.

As I zipped up my rucksack, he kept swimming out, alternating between a scrappy crawl and a breaststroke that made his head bob rhythmically. He angled right, towards the rock outcrop that marked the southern edge of the bay. Reaching it, he turned the corner and disappeared from view. Where was he going?

At the thirty-third step, I looked up and saw, coming down, another man, balding with clipped, greying hair. His short-sleeved shirt wasn't strictly Hawaiian but still garishly floral. His shorts were the same colour as his hair. I pretended not to notice him until he stood aside to let me pass. Puffing out his chest and snapping his heels together, he saluted.

'Morning, soldier. Change of personnel, eh?'

I muttered 'morning' back but didn't stop. He gave off a strong deodorant smell, somehow more intimate than BO would have been. Eyes lowered, I noticed his hairless shins, wafer-thin flip-flops, toenails in need of a trim.

At a corner further up, I looked down through the branches to the beach and water below. So this was why Ned had wanted rid of this beach, why he'd told me to get it done early. Napping on the stones definitely hadn't featured in his instructions.

The sound of clinking pebbles echoed up as the second man reached the bottom. Soon enough I spotted him, naked, stepping gingerly into the water. He took longer than the other man to fully get in, splashing cupped handfuls on to his torso and arms. Finally, he dived, arms stretched out, chin tucked into his chest. When he came up, he let out a garbled howl, kicking his legs and windmilling his arms. Not graceful but fast.

He swam out to the outcrop, skin white against the dark green water. I felt the thrill of getting away with something. In the changing rooms, letting your gaze linger even for a second on another boy's body had immediate consequences. But alone on those steps I was free to watch that naked bald man swim, as you might watch an unusual bird pass overhead, or a fine vintage car drive by. There was beauty in it, I suppose, though I couldn't have put it like that then. I only knew I was seeing something new, a part of the world previously obscured.

When I reached my bike, I found three yellow wild-flowers draped across the saddle.

'I said go early, didn't I?'

Ned was putting his bike in the shed, where I'd shoved mine two hours earlier. Since then I'd been stewing, rehearsing my complaint. But by the time I'd heard his tyres on the gravel, my anger had mostly faded. Still, I was determined to display my disgust.

'Is it every day?' I said.

He lifted his T-shirt to wipe his sweaty forehead. He was beginning to get hair on his torso, a fact that seemed to stretch the years between us. 'Two or three times a week. Weekdays. Eight thirty the first one comes down, the one with the Hi-Tecs. Then bang on twenty to nine, baldy appears.'

'How long . . . I mean, have you seen them swim back in?'

'Have I bollocks! Did you?'

'No way.' I screwed up my nose. 'Dirty old . . . gaylords.'

He looked amused. He had a way of making me feel clueless. 'Do you not want the job, then?'

'I don't want to get bummed senseless, that's for sure.'

His smirk broke into a proper laugh. He exited the shed and I followed him inside. 'They won't touch you, you muppet. Your balls haven't even dropped.'

I was glad he couldn't see me blush. 'Did they touch *you*?'

He stepped up and punched my arm, hard, catching it perfectly. 'Course they fucking didn't. And if they tried, I'd have caved in their skulls with a rock. I don't want to see it, is all. Don't want anything to do with it.'

'Me neither,' I said glumly, rubbing my arm.

Ned tossed thirty quid on the worktop—my first week's wages up front. 'Stay out of their way. And don't tell *anyone*.'

As if sharing grave news, Jacob announced that I'd been invited to 'supper'. Was this, I wondered, the same as dinner? Yes, it turned out, though it occurred closer to eight o'clock than six, when we usually ate at home. Still, I couldn't help imagining a kind of lofty ritual with dimmed lights, candles, classical music. I was nervous about the food—I couldn't stand salmon—my manners, topics of conversation, and being starved by the time we ate.

That evening, Jacob and I walked back from Beau Sejour after a solid two-hour shift spent experimenting with two-player mode. To our disappointment, but also grudging respect, Doom Viper had dealt with the extra pair of hands by deploying twice the normal quota of henchmen. The lesson was clear. If we were going to reach the castle and take him down, one of us was going to have to do it alone.

We were eating toffee bars, jaws working steadily, feeling the sticky pull on our teeth. I wanted Jacob to put me at ease about supper, but he seemed to be dreading it too.

'You're not a fussy eater, are you?' was all he said.

Classical music was indeed playing, though I couldn't see any candles. The kitchen was all gleaming worktops, silvery appliances, racks with pans and utensils hanging. Jacob's father, sporting a maroon-and-white-striped apron, monitored various simmering pots.

'Evening, chaps!' he said. 'This must be the famous Tom.' He shook my hand vigorously without squeezing too hard. 'Matthew Lovelong, welcome, welcome.' His high spirits surprised me—until now he'd only ever been an ominous, silent presence in the basement. 'Trust you like risotto, young man.'

The word was entirely new to me. 'Love it,' I said quickly, feeling Jacob eye me.

'How was the park? Jacob, fetch Tom some cordial. And set the table for me would you, darling?'

Dad never called me or my brother that. Wasn't it a woman's word? Or at least a word for addressing a woman? Jacob took two glasses from a cupboard. 'Lime or blackcurrant?'

'Don't mind.'

'Indecision!' said Matthew, loudly. 'A sure sign of weakness.' He stood at the stove, his back to us, a tall, thin man with a long neck covered with tiny, dark hairs. You could see where Jacob had got his big, flapping ears. The apron strap had messed up Matthew's collar, giving him a jaunty look. 'Deep down, Tom, you have a preference. Don't stifle your desires for some misguided notion of decorum.'

To my horror, my eyes began to sting. 'Blackcurrant, then?'

'Progress! Now rephrase as an assertion.'

'Blackcurrant, please.'

'Bravo!'

We had just sat down when I heard the front door slam, followed by heels kicked off with a theatrical groan. 'These people!' said a woman—Jacob's mother, I assumed. She went straight to the cupboard for a wine glass, filling it from a half-gone bottle of red, taking a couple of gulps before topping it up. Her loose, fair ponytail seemed casual compared with her white collared shirt, grey skirt, dark tights. 'Never have I encountered such incompetence, such lethargy, such –'

'Esther,' Matthew said, 'we've company.'

Her recovery was smooth. 'Tom! Of course! Forgive me ranting away. Welcome! What a pleasure. Are these oafs looking after you? I see you've got a drink, at least.'

She went on like that for a while, roaming from one thing to another, no response required. 'We're so pleased you and Jakie are hitting it off. Moving can be terribly difficult, especially at this age.' Jacob squirmed in his seat, huffing, shaking his head. The longer she talked, the more cracks you detected in the confidence and charm. 'Guernsey born and raised, eh? A thoroughbred Guern. Such a beautiful island, isn't it? Unique, really, yes.'

Matthew, at the stove, put his hand on her arm without looking up. She sipped from her glass, then put it down. 'Yes. I'll freshen up, shall I?'

As she padded upstairs, Matthew turned to smile at me. His eyebrows seemed unusually high and thin. 'Can you tell we don't often have guests, Tom? Jacob, give Leon a call, won't you?'

I watched Jacob dial *23. 'Supper,' he said, and hung up. The house had an internal phone system!

'Such *joie de vivre*,' Matthew said. 'Such *esprit de corps*.'

Soon I heard footsteps and voices descending. Esther and Leon, whoever he was, must have met on the stairs. I couldn't make out what was said over the music, but she sounded less chipper than before. I wondered if she was warning him I was there.

Did I know before I saw him who Leon would be? Now it seems I must have. But at the time it was a total surprise. He came in ahead of Esther, stocky and tanned, in his fifties, balding with clipped greying hair, floral shirt. My guts flipped. I wanted to jump up and run. He leaned over the Aga, inhaling, groaning with pleasure.

'Tremendous,' he said, clamping Matthew's shoulder with a meaty hand.

'One tries,' Matthew said.

Leon and Esther joined us at the table. 'Leon, meet Jacob's chum Tom.'

I tried to keep my eyes down but failed. He smiled at me as I caught a whiff of his deodorant.

'Well, well,' he said. 'If it isn't young Captain Soldiers'.'

Jacob and Esther looked between the two of us. Matthew began delivering steaming plates.

'Sorry?' I said. Playing dumb seemed the safest move.

'You're the litter man, no?' I detected a faint Cockney accent. 'Superhero in rubber gloves, bin sack for a cape. Eh? Or got the wrong bloke, have I? Tom here picks up rubbish down at Soldiers' Bay, one of my favourite spots for a morning splash. Victor Hugo used to swim there too, so I hear.'

'Really, Tom?' said Esther. 'How marvellous. You conscientious thing.'

'He gets paid,' Jacob put in sourly. 'His brother pays him to do his job.'

'Course he does,' said Leon. 'Deserves every penny too. That place is spotless.'

'Marvellous,' Esther said again. This time it sounded forced, like she was parsing the meaning of what she'd heard. She reached for her wine. Leon, I noticed, was drinking water. Matthew had the same.

'Do start,' he said. 'I trust it's not vile.'

'It's blinding,' said Leon.

The risotto looked like porridge with mushrooms and prawns thrown in—two things I wouldn't usually go near. But it didn't taste as bad as I feared. Mostly I noticed the cutlery—thick, smooth navy-blue handles—so heavy and shiny it made ours at home look like the plastic stuff in the Beau Sejour café.

I fielded questions about my parents. When I said my mother was from Nottingham, Leon said, 'Ay up, m'duck.' When I told them that my father worked for the States, all three of them looked at me, pausing in their chewing. Which department, Matthew wanted to know. When I said treasury, they all seemed to relax. I almost asked about his plays, but could sense Jacob willing me to keep my mouth shut. He was very quiet, eating fast, watching my half-full plate.

'Whatever happened to that red T-shirt?' Esther asked. 'Haven't seen it for weeks. I rather liked that one.'

Jacob said he'd lost it. How on earth does one lose a T-shirt? Probably left it in the changing room at swimming. So he'd walked home topless?

'I lose things there all the time,' I chimed in. 'Goggles, trunks, towels. You name it.'

She looked at me kindly.

'You boys should be swimming in the sea,' said Leon. 'Get out of all that piss and bleach.'

'May we be excused?' Jacob said.

As I watched him load his stuff into the dishwasher, my fork slid off my plate. Somehow I caught it on my socked foot and bent to pick it up. No one noticed any of it. Maybe that explained what I did next, which was to slip the fork into my mouth, cleaning it with my tongue, then place it into the front pocket of my hoodie. I slotted my plate, knife and glass into the rack and followed Jacob upstairs.

His room was bigger than mine, with a black sofa against one wall, plus TV, boombox and Mega Drive. He switched on the console and slumped miserably on to the cushions. As we waited for *Sonic* to load, Leon went by whistling, heading back upstairs.

'He's the lodger, in case you're wondering,' he said— snidely, I thought. 'He works with my dad.'

I nodded as if this was normal.

'Lots of people have lodgers,' he went on. 'We have the space—why not use it?' I'd never heard him say 'we' like that before. '*En famille* tenancies are actually encouraged by the States of Guernsey.' Now I could tell he was parroting. 'Yet another quirk of your medieval little rock.'

It wasn't the first time he'd made a comment like that. I hated it when he slagged off the island. Hated that French accent too. 'Is he your uncle or something, then?'

He shot me a look of pure disdain, then busied himself careening through level one.

'It's not *medieval*,' I said, eventually.

'How would you know? You've never lived anywhere else!'

'So? Living in London doesn't automatically make you better.'

He scoffed. 'If you don't think London's better than Guernsey, you're even more retarded than you look.'

The fork was in my pocket, cradled in one hand, and suddenly I wanted to drive it into his smug, ugly face. No wonder you get so much stick, I thought, you say whatever you want. I imagined siding with the bullies next time, calling him Salmon, Salmon Boy, punching and kicking as the crowd egged me on, leaving him a blubbing mess on the floor.

'I'm going,' I said.

'Off you go, then.' His eyes never left the screen.

Must be nice, I thought as I pedalled home, to choose your own friends.

Later that week, Ned came into my room. He was excited but trying to be cool.

'The plot thickeneth,' he said.

In the end, I'd told him about Leon. He had an

21

uncanny ability for gathering gossip—his network was extensive. If he'd found out on his own, he'd have killed me for not filling him in. And if word got out, it wouldn't look great for either of us.

'Well?' I said.

'Two things. First, according to Nifty's mum—who's heavily into musicals and panto and all that bollocks— Jacob's dad wrote these mental sex plays that caused, like, a sensation.'

'Sex plays.'

'As in the actors literally ploughed each other on stage. Not just bloke-on-woman either. Girl-on-girl, man-on-man—the works.'

'Nifty's mum said that?'

'She said "graphic polysexual acts". Anyway, it all got shut down after a few months. But by that point he— Jacob's dad, I mean—had become this cult figure. Because these plays were actually *amazing*.'

I tried to take this in. 'Two things, you said.'

He grinned, started pacing. 'So, you know how The Shark's uncle is in AA.'

'The car thing?'

There was that belittling look again. He told me what each A stood for. 'A few months ago, Jacob's dad and this Leon guy started turning up at the meetings. Supposedly, Leon is Jacob's dad's sponsor.'

'Meaning?'

'Meaning after all the kinky play shit went south—or maybe before, who knows—Jacob's dad hit the bottle, big time. And Leon took him under his wing.'

I remembered them sipping water at supper, Esther's teeth stained red.

'Actually, three things. The Shark's uncle reckons they moved here to get away from all the London madness, and brought Leon along to keep old Shakespeare off the sauce. Which means he's probably here without a permit.'

'Jacob said they're doing *en famille*.'

'But he's not actually *en* the *famille*, is he. He's loafing about in their loft and popping down to Soldiers' now and then for a blowie.'

'Gross.'

Ned stopped pacing. 'So what do you reckon?'

I shook my head. What did I reckon? In the week since supper, I'd been getting to Soldiers' even earlier. I hadn't been back to Jacob's, and he hadn't called. My *Silver Sabre* withdrawal was getting bad—sometimes I found myself thinking about the Zarnans. But no matter how pissed off I was at Jacob, playing without him still felt wrong.

'Is it Jacob's dad?' Ned said. 'The one who swims out first?'

I shook my head and wondered, not for the first time, who that other man was.

'But they're definitely bum chums, yes?'

'Jacob hates Leon, that's for sure.'

'No shit—Leon turned his dad gay then moved himself in. Well, is Jacob a mate?'

I thought about that. Ned and his friends were tight, more like brothers to each other than the two of us were. They called him Scarf—Scarfinger, Scarfy—and I wished I could call him that too. Jacob and I would never be like that. I remembered Beale kicking Jacob, burning his shirt. If Ned had been the one on the ground, his friends would have kicked Beale shitless. Chester too.

'Because if he's a mate,' he was saying, 'you've got to back him up. That's what mates do. You understand what I'm saying?'

At first, I didn't. But then, just like that, I decided I did.

That night, I couldn't sleep. The air was cool but I felt feverish. A demo reel played over and over in my head—spotlit figures on a stage, naked, sweat-drenched, twisted into depraved positions. Fanning themselves with folded programmes, audience members applauded politely as the actors thrashed and squealed. Then came a wet-haired man on a rock, stranded a long way out to sea, shivering, goosepimples on his scrawny arms, seagulls squawking and shitting at him. Finally, Esther and Jacob, huddled in the kitchen, candles all burned down, wax spilling and pooling as giggles echoed up from the base-ment below. Then back to the beginning.

The call is from destiny, Homer kept saying. Except in place of Homer's face, I saw my brother's. *Will you accept the charges?*

Finally, I switched on my desk lamp. I'd stuck a *Ghost-busters* sticker on the shade when I was eight and now Stay Puft grinned at me pitilessly. I opened my jotter and found a blank page. With my plastic Parker fountain pen, in cur-sive as unlike mine as I could manage, I began to write.

It didn't take long. At four-ish, as the birds were

starting, I tore the page out, folded it carefully into quarters and zipped it into the secret pocket of my rucksack. Seconds later I was asleep, sprawled on top of my Pac-Man duvet. When my alarm rang, my head felt packed with wet cement. But I dragged myself up. Once my parents had gone, I pinched an envelope and a stamp from the drawer in the kitchen, then scanned the phone book until I found what looked like the right department. It was in the building where my father worked, which stopped me for a minute. No, I decided, it didn't make a difference. In the same barely legible stranger's hand, I copied the address.

When I left, Ned was still in bed.

There was a post-box under the archway going into Fort George. As I went to drop the envelope, I paused. For years I'd been desperate for a nickname—was I really going to betray the man who'd finally given me one? All for a so-called friend I barely liked, who I was pretty sure didn't give two shits about me? I was too tired to think. My fingers opened and the envelope fell on to the others piled inside.

On the cliff path, at the top of the steps, I checked my Casio. Five past eight, still plenty of time. The sky was bright, practically cloudless, the sea calm, tide low. A ragged piece of polystyrene lay stranded on the gleaming wet sand. Shoebox-sized, by far the biggest thing I had found down there. I headed straight for it. Striding, I shrugged my rucksack off and pulled out my gloves and a black sack. Only once I'd bagged it did I turn and see him, up in the corner, sitting on the stones.

Leon.

He waved. I waved back and trudged up the beach.

'All right, Captain?' he said. His shirt that morning was brown and flower-free. His knees were up in front of his chest, arms wrapped loosely around them. From one hand hung a limp banana skin. 'Given you a shock, have I?'

I shook my head, but knew I must be pale.

'Looks like a few bits washed in with the tide. Pity more people don't make it down, eh? See what a fine job you're doing.'

'They come in the afternoon,' I said, not that I could prove it. 'Not everyone likes to swim so early.'

'Best time of day!' He looked out to sea, shaking his head as if freshly taken with it all. 'When I was a kid, we either went down the tracks to chuck stones at trains, or stood on the flyover and chucked them at cars. Most days, it was both. I'd've killed for a spot like this.' He looked at me and I saw he had something to say. 'Seeing Jacob later?'

I shrugged.

'Fallen out, haven't you. Moody little sod, he is. Has he said much to you? About me, I mean.'

I was moving stones around with my shoes. I said no. It wasn't a lie, but I knew he saw through it.

He sighed and stood, dropping the banana skin into my sack. 'Thing is, we're really making progress, Matthew and me. Really doing some quality work, but—it's tricky. With Esther, I mean. We had to fight like mad to get her to let me come with them, and she only agreed on the

condition that her precious little Jakie wasn't *disrupted*.'
He shook his head. 'He's a bloody teenager! What teenager doesn't mope about? But apparently my *presence*'—he
made quotes with his fingers—'is *unsettling* him.'

The Condor was heading out, on its way to Jersey or
Saint-Malo, stately, leisurely, trailed by a colossal wake.
In a few minutes, the waves would arrive, ten or twelve
crashing on to the sand.

'Maybe you can talk to him,' Leon said. 'Tell him I'm
not all bad. Tell him I'm only here for his old man's sake.'

I wanted very badly to look at my watch. Instead I
looked up, scanning the steps.

'Just you and me today, Cap'n.' He smiled. 'So? Help
a geezer out?'

I nodded.

'Good lad.' He ruffled my hair and I felt his fingers
slide down to my cheek, tapping gently twice. 'I'll let you
get back to it. Time for a dip, methinks. Get in there
before those waves arrive. Love a bit of turbulence,
don't you?'

I wandered off, head down, pretending to survey the
stones. My heart was galloping and my legs felt hollow.
The moment he splashed into the water, I made for the
steps.

After that, I stopped going down. Didn't tell Ned. Rode
my bike through the lanes for an hour each morning,
past our old primary school, green playing fields, sleepy
houses. Didn't tell him about the letter either. Every
time the phone rang, I was sure it would be Jacob, telling

me Leon was gone. Finally, two weeks since supper, eight days since I'd posted the letter, he called.

'I'm finishing it today.' He sounded sombre and adamant. 'Thought you might want to watch.'

'You've been *playing*? How far have you got?'

'To the castle.'

'You've seen him?'

'With my own two eyes.'

I felt sick. 'Is he—brutal?'

'He has his weaknesses. So?'

I stayed quiet to make it seem like I was thinking. But I was already pulling my trainers on and fumbling with the laces.

I found him sitting on the low wall that bordered the indoor rock garden. He looked older somehow. Dark rings around his eyes. The tight curls on his head had expanded, finally concealing his ears. He sat very upright and still, staring fixedly ahead.

'I brought pound notes,' I said, out of breath, 'in case we need change.'

He shook his head faintly, once. 'I'm doing it with twenty.'

'Pence?'

'I have to stay on the blue dragon when I'm crossing the drawbridge.'

'Into the castle?'

He gave me the look he normally saved for boys he particularly loathed. 'Into the garden fucking shed.'

I followed him into the arcade. A woman held her

toddler up to the *Out Run* steering wheel. Other than that, empty. The screens all danced and flickered. *Silver Sabre* waited faithfully in its corner.

In front of the machine, Jacob stretched—shoulders, neck, hands, hips—the way our swimming coach had us warm up poolside. He produced a single twenty-pence piece from his pocket, examined it, slotted it in and hit 'Start'.

'Good luck,' I said, wobblier than I'd have liked.

He dealt with level one perfectly, not sustaining a single blow. The sumo giants, once so daunting, he slaughtered with stunning ease. All through Lizard City he left piles of henchmen who turned to stone in death. The big pink knight at the end of level five he dispatched without resorting to magic. Occasionally, slyly, I studied his face. He blinked at standard intervals, impassive except for a steady flexing of his jaw. No obscenities, no groans.

The levels went by in a blur until Jacob reached the Devil's Road, both lives still intact. The skeletons with their shields and Samurai swords began assaulting him in numbers. Finally, he hit the 'Magic' button, bringing a giant raptor down out of the sky to vomit reams of fire. Two skeletons survived—he took them apart hand to hand. Level seven was done.

'Holy crap,' I breathed.

The final level started badly. Lyra was clubbed and flung to the ground by an ugly ginger dwarf. One life gone, one to go. Jacob's jaw tensed and relaxed. By now, a couple of kids were watching. One, chubby with a wedge, kept shouting 'Nice one!' and 'Whoa!' I glared until he got the hint.

There it was—the drawbridge. The blue dragon appeared, ridden by a blonde woman wearing even less than Lyra. Jacob knocked her off, sliced her up, made the dragon his. I was hardly breathing. Two huge pink knights guarded the threshold, their swords ten times longer than Lyra's own. Incredibly, Jacob saw them off without taking a hit. Suddenly, he was entering the castle.

The screen stopped scrolling. Lyra was in a hall with pillars, cobbled floors, coats of arms. Hanging by the ankles from thick metal chains were the king and his wife. Foot soldiers came rampaging into the hall. It took me a while to notice the pile of writhing snakes and the figure rising out of it, bigger and more menacing than the others. A massive blade materialized in his hands. His face was a mask with blackness for eyes.

'There he is,' I whispered.

Jacob threw what remained of his magic. After that, pure carnage. The way he wrenched and yanked at the joystick, the speed with which he hit the buttons—relish. One by one he took the henchmen down until only the overlord remained.

Lyra was still up on her fire-breathing dragon. Jacob let out a big, strained breath. His forehead got sweaty as more spectators gathered, seven or eight now, huddling. For a long time, he focused on defence, dodging the sacred sabre and leaping over fireballs. The longer he went without attacking, the more anxious I felt. But I knew he was biding his time.

At last, so fast that I barely saw it, he lunged the dragon forward, knocking Doom Viper down. After that, it was a matter of standing over him and breathing fire as he struggled back up. Eight, nine, ten times this happened. The timing had to be perfect. Jacob's head bobbed in a steady rhythm, three bobs between each burst of fire. The crowd hushed in anticipation.

Suddenly, the sabre flew high into the air. It came down spinning and wedged into Doom Viper's chest. Rivers of blood erupted as a wolfish howl rang out through the speakers.

It was over.

'Yes!' I cried, thumping Jacob on the back. 'Yes, yes, yes!'

He punched the console once with the side of his fist and let out a guttural snarl. He seemed enraged, relieved, ecstatic, shattered. Behind us there were murmurs of approval and unease.

When Lyra released the hostages, they hugged one another, completely ignoring the long-lost daughter come home to set them free. I expected a grand celebration, the Zarnans paying tribute to their saviour. I expected Lyra to take a bow, or be brought some reward, or refreshments at least. But she simply stood apart, alone, unnoticed, as her parents embraced and the screen went black.

'Is that it?' Jacob said.

'Huh. Seems like –'

'No one cares? No one says thank you or well fucking done?'

With a stiff-necked shake of the head, he turned and strode out of the arcade, legs doing their half-shackled thing. I hurried after him, out into the daylight. He marched away across the park. He kicked over a bin, sending Cornetto wrappers and Walkers packets flying. He walked in big arcs and tight circles, muttering, gesturing.

Suddenly, he headed for the far benches, where two people sat. With a jolt I realized the distant figures were Beale and Chester. No girls this time, just Bubbles and Cheese. Next moment, I was sprinting.

I got there in time to see Jacob drag Beale up by the collar. Beale shoved him away. Jacob landed a punch close to Beale's right eye with a horrible, bony pop. Beale went down but rolled, scrambling back up.

'Give it to me!' Jacob screamed. It wasn't the red Quiksilver one, but that didn't seem to matter.

My eyes met Chester's. Neither of us could intervene without implying our friend was in trouble. It was either stand back and watch, or fight among ourselves. His smirk confirmed that he knew as well as I did how that would likely go. I felt relieved, almost grateful.

Which made it all the more surprising to find myself careening at him head first, slamming my skull into the centre of his chest before he could even flinch.

We went down tangled, limbs scrabbling. The wind gushed out of his lungs and I smelled his smoky breath, his Lynx body spray, mixed with soil and grass. Jacob kept repeating his manic demand, but I couldn't see what was happening. Chester, rasping, was trying to gouge my eyes, so I jerked my head away and brought my elbow down. A tingly pain ran down my forearm and up into my shoulder, so intense I failed to notice for a moment that I'd caved in Chester's nose.

Blood like the blood from Doom Viper's chest came spurting out. Instantly it was all over me, my neck, hands, lips. I was growling, spitting, wriggling away. Chester howled, hands to his face, curling on his side. I staggered up. Beale had Jacob pinned but Jacob was still screaming. A great sob was building in my chest and I could feel my bottom lip quivering. The only thing I could think to do was kick Beale in the balls, which I did, from behind, hard as I could. With a yelp he slumped off Jacob, who immediately set about tearing off Beale's shirt. Beale barely struggled, face screwed up, groaning and half puking on the grass.

We stood over them, panting, sweaty, blood-spattered, stunned. The whole thing had lasted less than thirty seconds.

'*By doze!*' Chester wailed.

'Fuck your nose!' said Jacob.

My ears rang. My elbow felt like it had been chiselled. Jacob was wide-eyed, neck veins bulging, T-shirt bunched in his right fist. Glistening scratches marked one of his cheeks and grass stains covered his clothes. I thought he might offer some final, defiant remarks. But he only sniffed and spat and walked away. I followed. Our strides kept widening until we were running—sprinting—for home.

Over the years, I've told various versions of all this. Parts of it, anyway. If vintage arcades come up, I'll mention my friend who completed *Silver Sabre* on only twenty pence. If someone brings up the south-east bays, I'll hint at what used to go on down at Soldiers', and who knows, maybe still does. I'll spend theatre intervals sharing what I know about the late, great Matthew Lovelong. And last year, when I heard from my brother that Jacob was in a Limehouse methadone clinic, I told him about that message from William S. Sessions, a message we saw so often that summer we stopped seeing it altogether.

At the park's edge, we slowed. I tried to calm down. You didn't break a guy's nose and get away with it. As for what I'd done to Beale . . . But Jacob seemed fine. Probably he'd already worked out, as I eventually would, that Beale and Chester could never let on what had really happened. He handed me the T-shirt to wipe off Chester's blood. As he opened the front door, in place of the usual quiet, I heard raised and strained voices.

Finger to lips, Jacob closed the door silently behind us. We froze. His father and Leon were in the kitchen. One of them was pacing.

'Put it down,' Leon said. 'Let's try and think.'

'I knew it!' Matthew cried. 'I knew one of these bloody inbreds would stick their little oar in.'

'But we don't actua–'

'*It's been brought*, it says. *It's been brought to our attention*. Which means some miserable, interfering shit took it upon themselves . . .'

I heard liquid swilling in a glass, a post-gulp gasp, the *thunk* of a bottle slammed down. I looked at Jacob, but his eyes were down.

'I'm not going to take it away from you,' Leon said. 'Listen to me. You have to be the one. You've worked so bloody hard, M. You've done so bloody *well*.'

I heard a moan, a throaty snort. Matthew was sobbing.

Jacob looked at me then. One of the scratches on his cheek was already scabbing over. To this day I don't know if it occurred to him—then, or ever—exactly what I'd done. I never told him. Never got the chance. In September, when school started up again, the house-master told us that Jacob was now boarding at a school in Devon. By Christmas, his parents had left too—so The Shark's uncle said.

At that moment, in the hallway by the big oak-framed mirror, his only concern was getting me out. I wanted to tell him I wasn't shocked, that none of it mattered to me. But there was no time.

As Jacob very carefully turned the latch and ushered me on to the steps, I thought I heard Leon say, 'You're going to be fine.' But a noisy old car went by, spewing black exhaust.

The door closed. I was alone. My bike, I realized, was still locked up outside Beau Sejour.

I've told myself different versions too, versions with better endings. In one, I decline Ned's offer, waste the summer sleeping in. In the next, I turn down that supper invitation and never learn Leon's name. In another, I drop that letter into my black sack instead of the post-box. These alternatives all bring some comfort. But the one I like best is the one where I go down to Soldiers' first thing—early doors, as Ned would say—the day they kick Leon off the island. I reach the bottom of the steps at twenty to nine. I note the plastic bag, black shirt and jeans, the orange towel and Hi-Tecs stowed neatly on the stones. I watch the Condor sail out ahead of its wake. I strip off and brave the cold and swim out around the rocks to tell the shivering man that his friend, I'm so sorry, your friend isn't coming.

2. Exactly What You Mean

The house seemed fine until she noticed the trampoline. A cheap old thing more weathered than worn out, it stood in the corner of the sunlit lawn, taunting Melissa as she smoked on the porch, watching bees rove from flower to flower. Without hesitation, she blamed its presence on her younger sister, Nicola, who had arranged this trip for the two of them, only to bail with days to spare so she could go instead to Dubrovnik with a boyfriend who, in Melissa's opinion—she had met him twice—was suspiciously polite. Suve was his name, short for something. Who could remember what?

Shirtless men were erecting a marquee in the garden next door, owned, so the ring-bound handbook claimed, by the Zeldins, a 'delightful' couple with two small children. She checked her BlackBerry—no signal. Isolation was already enveloping her. She asked herself aloud if she mightn't like a drink.

Monségur was fifteen minutes away—she had passed through it on her drive from the airport. In the supermarket now she was reckless, selecting multiple cheeses and bottles of wine, strange vegetables, slabs of unidentified meat, tubes of extravagant cookies. This week of seclusion in the vineyards of Bordeaux had been

conceived as a kind of detox, but that was before it had become a solitary affair—one featuring an old trampoline and a party to which she wasn't invited.

In her teens, trampolining had been her thing. At the encouragement of her PE teacher, Mr Platt, she'd competed in regional meets, qualifying at sixteen for the nationals. Popular girls, her sister included, taunted her for spending more time with Mr Platt—a forty-something unmarried Brummie, tall, fair-haired, with piercing eyes, owner of a burnt-orange VW Westfalia as well as a silver Kawasaki—than with boys her own age. But the truth was, she thrived on his attention. As much as it was a discipline, a sport, trampolining was also a performance, and she knew no elation to match that of executing a flawless routine as Mr Platt watched with sombre approval, arms crossed, nodding in his shabby tracksuit.

Her commitment had been total until, during one of four weekly after-school sessions, she'd lost concentration when her coach's interest diverted visibly to a younger girl stretching on a nearby mat. That fall demolished her right knee. Even after surgery and months of physio, the doctors were adamant. Mr Platt said it was a terrible waste. Heart-breaking, he said. But he'd already moved on, wrapped up in his latest protégée. That was fifteen years ago. She hadn't set foot on a bounce mat since, though her recent attempts to forget about Jonathan had brought to mind that leaden-legged feeling of stepping down and walking away.

She texted Nicola from outside the supermarket—*Arrived in one piece, house gorgeous*—then sat in her rented

Fiat for a while watching French wives load their own cars with groceries. One dropped a bag and shrugged as three oranges rolled away. Melissa waited for her sister to reply, fighting the urge to text Jonathan also, six weeks now since his letter. *Flora is making me run the marathon with her*, he'd written. *In other words, she knows.* The familiar childish scrawl had prompted an unwelcome surge of affection. *I hope you realize how much you have meant.* She hadn't written back but had added the letter to her collection of trinkets from their time together, a pathetic array of receipts and stolen cutlery she wasn't yet ready to throw away.

Today was Saturday. The marathon was tomorrow. The instructions to her sister had been simple—get me out of London that weekend! By which she meant please save me the indignity of clinging to a railing, crushed by the cheering hordes, fighting for a glimpse of him sweating beside his wife. By the time her phone buzzed, the supermarket was closed. *Well done, Dubrovnik a-mah-zing too! Suve says hi, how are you.*

Twice a week they had gone to her flat after work and spent an hour or two together, watching television afterwards, wallowing in bed like a real couple. With her, Jonathan had laughed at the same American sitcoms he sneered at his wife for enjoying. He was liked by his staff, well-dressed but not showily so, stern when necessary but generous and approachable. His glasses were trendy, if a touch young for him, and every Monday he went to the barber for a trim and cut-throat shave. For most of her five months as his assistant, she had also been his mistress, a word he used often and to which she outwardly objected, though the prim authority it granted her always inspired a little thrill. She would have preferred 'lover', a term she knew he could never use. She went down on him once in his office, in the middle of the day, with phones ringing and door unlocked, because he teased her that she didn't have the nerve. After that, it had all started to lose its sheen. She knew he would never leave Flora, wasn't even sure she wanted him to. There were children too, three teenagers. The two daughters beamed out of frames on his desk—pretty, privileged, the sort of bitches she'd hated at school.

Near the end, he'd asked her to name her favourite perfume. He'd come back from lunch with a small bag from Selfridges, thick black paper embossed with gold. Closing the door, she turned to him with a conspiratorial smile, the thought of which now made her want to throw up. 'Okay for tonight?'

He shook his head without looking up, typing on his laptop. 'Anniversary. Two days ago, in fact.'

She gave notice that same week. On her last day, the whole floor gathered while he wished her well at a rival agency. Don't give away our secrets, he said. Everybody laughed falsely, guiltily, clutching their little plastic cups of Prosecco. So they'd known all along. Owen, the IT geek who'd been obsessed with her for years. Sharon McGrath, the miserable cow who'd tried to pinch her Valentine's flowers that time. Everybody.

One of the other PAs gave her a long hug. Don't look

so blue, the woman said, we'll all keep in touch. You're on LinkedIn, aren't you?

The marquee party sounded strange, surrounded by so many empty acres. She wondered how far into the vines she'd have to walk to escape it. She imagined the guests—healthy and tanned, grinning in the flow of their idyllic lives—and lit another cigarette. By the time darkness settled, the wine bottle was empty.

A knock at the front door woke her. She was sprawled on the sofa, lamps on, laughter still audible. The man on the porch stood a polite distance back in a crisp shirt, chinos, expensive leather sandals. His thick dark hair was neatly cut and his teeth caught the light from inside as he smiled. He was stubbly, in need of a cut-throat blade. One eyebrow ran into the other.

With a firm handshake he introduced himself as Vincent Zeldin, the neighbour. The handbook said he was an orthodontist, and she felt he somehow looked like one. She ran her fingers through her sleep-flat hair as he apologized for the noise, gaze flicking beyond her into the house. 'You are alone?'

'My sister went to Dubrovnik instead.' When he asked if she'd like to join them in the marquee—my birthday, he said—she indicated her outfit, her face. '*Merci*, but I'm—a mess.'

He repeated the word and shook his head. 'You are perfect!'

After he left, she went straight to the mirror, adjusting her hair, sucking in her cheeks, pulling back her shoulders.

Eyes too close together, wide nostrils, shiny forehead, dull and crooked teeth. Her figure was better—better than Nicola's, anyway. *Getting a bit top-heavy for the trampo, Mel,* Mr Platt had said, once.

There was a crease down one side of her face from the sofa.

'Perfect,' she said.

In shuttered darkness she woke with a headache and no idea of the time. On the white walls were mosquitoes she had killed, paint stained with smudges of their blood mixed with hers. The garden was wet from half-remembered morning rain and grey clouds packed the sky. She ate a tube of cookies on the sofa and tried not to think about the marathon. Later she strolled barefoot around the lawn. Dead apples, figs and plums lay scattered beneath their trees.

She approached the trampoline as if it were a seething hive. The mat was slick, the springs rusty. She mounted and for a while stood completely still, feeling the material stretch under her feet. With faint movements of her toes she began to bounce, hardly breaking contact. Dizziness washed over her. In her knee, not pain so much as the memory of it. The rain started up again.

At four thirty, she opened a bottle of red. On the coffee table sat various big books—*The Times Atlas of the World*, a wine encyclopaedia. One was all photographs of Africa, taken by someone called Bill Pointer. Black and white, landscapes mostly, some obligatory elephants and tribesfolk. It was the kind of book she wanted to like but had no idea how to read. Did you just sit and stare at the pictures, waiting for a feeling to emerge? Were you supposed to pick up the phone and donate to UNICEF or whatever? She got halfway through and gave up, opting instead for the guestbook.

The entries dated back to 2003. Everyone remarked on the splendid weather, the incredible walks, the gardening. Most had taken trips to *bastides* and *châteaux*, rented bikes, ridden horses, played golf. *Everything was perfect*, someone wrote, *exactly what we needed*.

The morning walk to Taillecavat, longer than the handbook implied, took her past fields of sunflowers and vines slathered in light. Cows came to greet her, lowing over the wire, and in a garden there were tiny chicks, stumbling and chirping, yellow down ruffled by the breeze. As she entered the empty streets of the village, a dog trotted out, barked once and disappeared.

The bakery was closed. *Fermé le lundi*, the sign said. She wondered if Jonathan had gone into work, if he could walk after yesterday. He probably had blisters all over his feet. She imagined bursting them for him with one of those little olive forks—there were two in her collection, lifted from their first lunch date.

Her phone buzzed. *Guess who got engaged!* She gazed through the window at the empty shelves, trying to compose a response. *The bakery is closed*, she wrote. Something more was needed but she couldn't think what. She sent it like that and dropped the phone into her bag.

As she walked back, a woman came jogging towards her in a vest and little shorts. They smiled as they passed. Before Melissa reached the house, the woman approached again, this time from behind, out of breath, her vest damp with sweat. She slowed, offered a clammy hand and introduced herself as Claudine, the neighbour. She looked twenty-six or -seven, with blue eyes and covetable cheekbones and the figure, Melissa thought, of a mother trying to get back to her best. There was desperation in her friendliness, a glimpse of endless hours at home with the kids.

'Our party is not bad for you? I send Vincent maybe to bring but you sleep, I think.'

Melissa blinked. 'Oh. Yes, I was very—I mustn't have heard the door.' Claudine invited her in for coffee. 'Thank you but I have some work to do.' Why was she lying to this woman?

Later she looked over the bookshelf in one of the bedrooms. Her eye was caught by the name—Marguerite Duras—on a slim spine. *The Lover.* Duras was the name of a nearby town, one that both guest-book and handbook talked up. She pulled the book out and read the blurb. The word 'devastating' appeared twice. She put it back on the shelf, picked a dog-eared thriller instead.

Sprawled on a lounger, straps off her shoulders, she read in the sun. After a while she heard voices and car doors through the trees and sat up to see Vincent waving off Claudine and the children. When they'd gone, he began to mow the lawn, his chest and shoulders thick with hair, hint of a gut above his orange shorts. She stood, removed her sunglasses, pulled her straps up.

The rusty springs creaked under her weight, the mat hot against her soles. She began slowly, building momentum as Mr Platt had taught her, creeping higher and higher as the confidence seeped back. With each leap, the landscape opened up. Beyond the trees, Vincent pushed his mower. She went through some basic moves—somersault, straddle, twist-to-seat. Each felt tremendous. Why had she deprived herself for so long? Her hair was in her eyes— she hadn't tied it back—but she sensed him watching, one hand up to block the glare, and the watching urged her on.

Her strength soon started to fade, her thighs burning. Still, she went into another somersault, in pike this time, digging what life she could from the old springs. But the take-off felt wrong, her trajectory off. Before she was halfway over, she knew.

The immediate stillness after impact was shocking, the sudden pungent earth against her cheek. Her vision was all sparks as she rolled over, whimpering. Vincent was there, crouching, his hand on her forehead, smiling like a man trained to inflict one pain with the intention of easing another. He lifted and carried her inside, his damp chest hair soft against her skin, setting her down on a familiar sofa strewn with cookie crumbs.

He fetched a glass of water, perching on the coffee table as she sipped. 'You are okay,' he said. He looked older than the other night—mid to late thirties. His hair was pushed back off his sweat-slick forehead as he gestured towards the trampoline outside. 'Wow! Fantastic!'

She shifted, wincing. There was pain in several places, but the worst of it was in her knee, the jagged agony deep in the joint as familiar as the voice of a sibling. He traced his fingers down the leg from hip to ankle. 'No fracture, I think.'

'It's my knee.' She drank the rest of the water. 'I know what it is.' She could smell him, the smell of a man's body. Her breathing had steadied and her head was clearing, but it all felt like a dream. 'Thank God you were here.'

He seemed to know it had all been for him. She glanced away as if caught out, but the pretence was paper-thin. As he took the glass and began to stand, she put her hand on his knee. He paused, then leaned to kiss her, on the forehead, cheek, mouth. She tasted sweat around his lips, coffee on his tongue, feeling a rush of something—the absence of remorse, perhaps. He knelt, tugging her bikini bottoms down and placing them on the low table like a surgical instrument he might need again. Sunlight in the room, his head between her thighs—too much. She closed her eyes. He rose off his knees, his mouth finding hers.

Afterwards, she looked away as he pulled up his shorts, straightening her bikini top. He handed her the bottoms like they were a cup to spit in. '*Voilà.*'

The mower started again. The blanket underneath her needed washing, and she carried it, limping, down to the machine. In the corner of the basement was a plastic paddling pool that she took out to the garden behind the house. She found a hose connected to a rusty old tap and, with barely an inch of cold water in the bottom, she stepped gingerly into the pool and lay down, letting it fill slowly around her until it overflowed.

The road to Duras wound through neat swathes of forestry, sunflowers, vineyards, weathered old houses. The town was a warren of cobbled streets on a hill. On the roof of the *château* she lingered for an hour, looking out over the countryside, her knee throbbing despite painkillers. She tried to locate the house in the distance but could not.

A plaque at the edge of Place Marguerite Duras seemed to say that the little square had been renamed for the writer after her death in 1996. Fifteen years ago, Melissa thought, the same year she'd hurt her knee. Outside a shaded café in the corner, a waitress greeted her, a big woman in her sixties with thin greying hair and glasses on a string around her neck.

'Marguerite Duras?' Melissa said, indicating the empty square.

The woman's face brightened and she began to speak quickly, leaving Melissa to pluck translatable fragments from the stream—writer, very sad, alcoholic, Vietnam, famous, Nazis, sex, death. Then she switched unexpectedly to English: 'You 'ave read *The Lover*, yes?'

'Oh, yes,' Melissa said. 'Devastating.'

She drove on to Eymet, another *bastide* town with ancient walls and the same empty afternoon indolence. At another café she tried to write a postcard, but the platitudes wouldn't come. She imagined sending one to Jonathan's house, Flora presenting him with it at dinner.

Stalls were setting up for an evening market. In the end she wrote *Wish you were here*, dropping the card unaddressed and unstamped into the post-box she passed as she limped back to the car.

She was halfway home when her phone began to ring, its unexpected melody startling her. Pulling off the road on to the gravelled shoulder, she dug the thing out of her handbag.

'Have you heard?' her mother said, unusually shrill.

'I got a text, yes.'

'Really? From who?'

They were talking about different things. Four women, former pupils from the eighties and nineties, were pressing charges against Mr Platt, citing various incidents in the changing rooms and in the back of his camper. The news had just broken locally—he still worked at the school and Bookham was scandalized.

'Did he ever . . .' Her mother's voice got quieter. 'You'd say, wouldn't you, love? If he'd ever done anything to you?'

'Never,' she said.

A car went past. Through its rear windscreen, she saw two little girls looking back, sticking out their tongues, faces screwed up. Her mother asked if she was surprised. She watched until the car disappeared around the corner.

'Not surprised, exactly. Maybe disappointed.'

'Yes,' her mother said, 'I know what you mean.'

Morning, her last full day at the house. In the corner of her room, a spider hung in its web, surrounded by offspring, new overnight. Dozens of them, tiny things suspended in the gauzy mesh.

Around noon, lying out in the garden, she heard what sounded like a motorcycle tearing down a distant stretch of road. She imagined a silver Kawasaki, chassis glinting in the sun, until the whine was suddenly oppressively loud and as close as if it were inside her head.

The swarm surged up from behind the far trees, a teeming mass coming directly towards her.

In an instant, she was on her feet and sprinting across the lawn, barely aware of the pain in her knee, not breathing, feeling the sound in pursuit, through the trees separating the houses and on into the Zeldins' garden, to an open door and through that, slamming it behind her and moving down a hallway into a kitchen, where she yanked shut one open window after another. Only then did she spin and see Claudine at the sink and two children at the table.

'Bees!' she screamed. 'Bees are coming!'

The baby girl began to wail. The boy, two or three years old, covered his ears with his hands, squirming in his chair, the Lego blocks in his fists clattering to the tiles. Claudine seemed frozen, watching Melissa with wide eyes, but then she stepped into her path, shouting in French to stop, relax. Melissa circled the table, grabbing at her hair, panting, trying to calm down. Things began to come into focus, the throbbing in her knee asserting itself. Seeing she had frightened the children, she forced a smile that seemed only to worsen her effect.

The baby kept howling, and Claudine picked her up.

'The bees are not bad,' she said. 'They only search for new place.'

Oh, Jesus, she was in her bikini. Melissa folded her arms across her chest, then put her hands over her eyes and apologized. Claudine, her touch unexpectedly gentle, pulled her hands away. Melissa mumbled again that she was sorry and moved towards the door.

'Please, stay! This little monster will sleep now, yes? *Es-tu prête pour une petite sieste maintenant, ma chérie?*' The French woman pulled out a chair and gestured for Melissa to sit. '*Jean, s'il te plaît sois gentil avec madame, okay?*' This she directed at the boy, who uncovered his ears reluctantly and fumbled again with his Lego. He had curly brown hair and a round face, a smudge of food on his chin. Something about his roaming gaze troubled Melissa until she realized—he couldn't see her. As the two of them sat, she watched him, unsure whether to speak. He ignored her absolutely. The longer it went on, the more exposed she felt.

When Claudine returned, she slipped a flimsy floral dress over Melissa's shoulders. '*Voilà.*'

They ate cheese and bread, thin stringy ham, grated carrot, endive. They talked about bees, about life in London and life there, about the children, Jean's blindness, work, the house.

'So you 'ave nice man at 'ome?'

Melissa shook her head. 'My friends are all coupled up, though, having babies. Even my little sister's getting married. I don't think I can stand another wedding.'

'But always there are men at weddings, no?' Claudine

winked and for a dizzy moment Melissa felt that she would tell this woman everything—how her husband had kissed the artless tattoo on her hip as if it were a graze on a child's palm, how he had torn down her bikini top and clawed at her breasts, growled French filth into her willing ear—she would blurt it all out and this woman, this mother, would only shrug and wink.

When Vincent came home not long after four, Melissa saw him flinch. Claudine introduced her and explained about the bees. He laughed uncertainly. 'Your leg is much better?'

She felt her eyes widen. 'Oh!' She dared not glance at Claudine but was sure she detected a pause in her movements, maybe a slight frown. Vincent's face warped into a weak, fearful grin. 'Much better,' she said, 'thanks.'

'You will stay for dinner?' he said quickly.

She declined. In English, Claudine asked him to walk Melissa back and check the place for bees. After a pause in which she saw his mind working, he picked up Jean and with the boy in one arm ushered her out the door.

'You don't have to do this,' she muttered, two paces behind.

'No problem!' His voice was unrecognizable. 'Jean is fight the bees, eh, Jean?'

The child only blinked, head lolling drowsily. They passed under the washing line where the sofa blanket still swung in the breeze. At the far side of the porch, he stopped. '*D'accord!* No bees 'ere, eh, Jean? *Pas de abeilles mauvaises?*'

She stepped into the house through the open glass

doors and turned to face the two of them. Vincent's eyes betrayed some kind of plea. The child hung in his left arm, glazed eyes flickering.

'I need to give you this dress,' she said quietly.

Frowning, he swallowed, his voice low now too. 'Dress?'

'Your wife's dress.'

'Ah.' His mouth sounded dry. 'Yes.'

He was diminishing, there in front of her. His helpless gaze streamed into her, seeming to lift, to fill her up. Slowly, eyes still locked on his, she pulled the dress up over her head and held it bunched in her hand. Standing in her bikini, she saw the gaze drift down. After a moment, she reached behind to unfasten the clasp, tilting her shoulders so the straps slid down and the top dropped silently. The faintest nod. With the child looking through her into the dark room behind, she tugged the bottoms down to the tiles, flicked them away and straightened. Breeze on her skin, holding out the dress, waiting for him to take it.

Vincent raised his free arm, reached for her breast. Stepping back, she watched his head drop, fought to steady her hand. She held out the dress and closed her eyes, hoping when she opened them to find herself alone.

3. Penny on the Wells

She appeared the summer we finished school, the summer we were due to jump the Wells. Alexis De Lisle came home from Clifton and got back together with Nifty Newton. Those two had been on and off since we were fifteen. Alexis had gone away to boarding school for sixth-form, leaving poor Nifty to suffer the mythology of what went on in such establishments. The Shark was the worst for that. 'Girl-on-girl orgies,' he would say. 'And that's the warm-up. That's until the rugby team arrives.' We all knew he was spouting, but still. Nifty hadn't been totally faithful himself, but I was less interested in all of that than in the new friend Alexis brought home for the summer.

Penny had long, straight, dark hair, a tiny upturned nose, a little gap between big white front teeth. She knew everything and cared about nothing. She'd been all over with her parents—Goa, Turkey, the Caribbean—and planned to spend the next year in Kenya, on a family friend's farm. To me, she was a glimpse of what the world out there promised, with its currencies and dialects, etiquettes and rituals, its landscapes and strange, delicious foods. Kenya? My adolescent mind was awash—bikini-clad Penny throwing raw meat to lions, or lifted in a ball gown by an elephant to ride on its leathery back. I was young, you understand, young and besotted. After Kenya, English at Cambridge.

One hot day that July, a group of us went down to Petit Port. Penny, ignoring the others as they warned her how cold the south-coast water got, wanted to swim. Of course, I volunteered, forcing down a shriek at the chill as we ran in. We swam a way out and soon found ourselves surrounded by bass, their slick grey backs catching the light at the surface. She yelped in surprise and grabbed hold of me. My arm was around her and I could feel her ribs under my fingers, her tight goosepimpled skin. When she splashed away, I swam obediently behind.

Instead of going back to the beach she headed for a little clump of rocks, fifty metres further out and half-way around to the next bay. 'Where are you going?' I called out, ruing the whiny note in my voice.

'On a mission!'

The water got colder the deeper we went. I'd won medals for swimming, but that was in the pool—this felt very different. Penny was a strong swimmer, though, reaching the rocks before me and struggling to clamber up, trying different holds on the steep sides.

'Boost me up, will you?' Treading water, I made a stir-rup with my hands and positioned myself to give her a lift. It worked perfectly, first time, and she let out a whoop, waving to our friends far away on the sand. Then I had to get myself up. It took several aborted attempts and earned me a pair of grazed knees. The saltwater stung, but I pretended not to notice as I hopped across to the flat section of rock where Penny already lay sunning, eyes shut. I sat cross-legged beside her, fighting to control my shivering. Her nipples were stiff under her black bikini, but otherwise she didn't seem to feel the cold. I tried not to stare.

'Lie down, won't you?' she said. 'The rock's lovely and warm.'

I wondered what the boys were thinking. No matter what I told them later, they would either call bollocks or rip me for bottling. I wasn't cocky enough to think she had dragged me out there to seduce me, but still I felt some pressure to make the most of the situation. I tried to think of something to say. My two drunken house-party fumbles with Anne-Marie Groves had hardly prepared me for this. Penny seemed at ease in the silence— I was desperate to fill it. In my head I was screaming at myself. *Say something, dickhead!*

'You get a lot of orgies at Clifton?'

I heard myself say it, and it hurt. I wanted to leap off the rock. I started to mumble an apology.

'It's not in the timetable, if that's what you mean,' she said. 'There's no Orgy Club meeting on Wednesday afternoons.'

I laughed eagerly, then muttered something about The Shark spreading rumours. She didn't seem to care. I vowed to stay quiet. The rock wasn't quite as flat as it seemed and bumps dug into my hips and back. Way above us, a tiny white jet dragged its contrail across the blue sky. Finally, she said, 'Did Nifty cheat on Lex while she was away?'

'Not to my knowledge,' I said, too quickly.

'Good answer. I don't actually care, though. I mean, she was snogging and shagging like mad.'

This was news. Nifty had strayed only when he and Alexis were 'off', and even then, he never did anything more serious than a bit of groping in a dark corner or two. Now it seemed like The Shark's imagination might not have been so wild after all. But what struck me was how casually Penny had betrayed her friend, how carelessly she had confided in me. I felt inspired to bring up something she had mentioned in the pub a few nights earlier.

'So you're sworn off men for a while?'

She rolled over on to her front, resting her head on her folded arms, facing me. There was a faint white crust around her eyebrows where the saltwater had dried. 'That's the plan,' she said. 'Celibate for a year. No more Naughty Penny.'

Pity, I couldn't bring myself to say. Then, maybe because I'd failed to rise to her provocation, she unfolded one arm and laid it across my chest. A casual gesture but, to me, sensational. I lay there, paralysed. Her skin felt warm on my cold chest. I wanted to know if her eyes were closed but didn't dare look.

By the time I decided to put my hand on hers, it was too late. She stood, stepped to the edge of the rock and, without so much as pausing to check the depth, dived in smoothly and swam towards the beach, her strong kicks stirring up a steady wake. For a moment, I stayed where I was, eyes screwed shut, fists clenched at my sides. Then

I jumped in after her, bloody knees smarting, and tried to catch up.

On a Saturday eleven years later, I flew home. My father picked me up in his shiny new Beemer. The car was too flash for him and he knew it. He drove like it was due back at the showroom in an hour.

'How's the Big Smoke?' he said.

'Still there.' I felt, actually, like a chunk of gristle spat out by the city. For weeks, I'd been waking booze-sick and sleep-deprived, standing under the dribbling shower till one of my housemates hammered on the door, cramming myself into the airless Tube, arriving at my desolately tidy desk for another day of online Scrabble. The previous month, I'd made only one sale, an ex-council dump in Kennington that went for no more than it was worth. Everyone was saying the market was ready to tank, the banks were going to need bailing out. Credit crunch, they were saying, massive recession. Doom was in the air like exhaust fumes over rush-hour Euston Road. I was glad to get away, even for the night.

'Looking forward to the wedding?' Dad said.

I wasn't about to give him the whole story. Even if I had, he wouldn't really have listened—too busy trying not to scratch his car. But the truth was I'd been eager for this day to arrive ever since Nifty and Alexis had got engaged in Val-d'Isère on New Year's Eve. 'Should be a laugh.'

He drove me straight to the care home. You won't go otherwise, he said, which was true. The place smelled like piss and disinfectant, with a hint of boiled cabbage. Walking down the muggy corridor, catching unwanted glimpses through open doors, I felt the usual urge to fling myself through the nearest sealed window. We found my grandmother in her chair, staring into space, television roaring in the corner. My father switched it off and Grandma turned. Her cheeks were almost comically pink, her white hair thin and clumpy. On her navy-blue cardigan there were three distinct food stains, one the shape of a seahorse. A glint of recognition passed over her face as I bent and put my arms around her. She used to be pretty sturdy, but she'd been shrinking ever since Granddad died, four years back. It used to be like hugging a tree. Now it was like holding a sack of leaves.

'Ned's home for a wedding,' my father said. Grandma perked up and then was visibly annoyed when she realized I wasn't the groom. When I was younger, she'd asked about girls ('Any feisty ones on the scene?'), but lately that had stopped—probably because I never brought any back to visit. 'You can't muck about indefinitely,' she'd say. She'd obviously given up hope of seeing me hitched before she died. My brother too, though for different reasons. According to Tom, the last time he'd paid Grandma a visit, she'd asked if his flatmate Russell was 'keeping the bed warm'. He was fairly pissed off about that, but I thought it was sad. Trying to come to terms with something untrue seemed a waste of resources for a woman with so few left.

'How's Tommy getting on?' she said, like she was reading my thoughts.

'Good, I think. He left the museum. He's doing walking tours now.' I saw that she didn't follow. 'He takes people around London, telling them about the history or the buildings or what-have-you.'

'And your mother?' She'd always been fond of Mum, who used to send her long letters from Nottingham when she first moved back up there after the divorce. Still did, actually, though not as often. Dad complained at first, but she told him it was none of his sodding business and, besides, Lucy was still the mother of her grandsons, wasn't she? I said she was fine, though I hadn't been up to Nottingham for nearly a year.

My father stepped in to say we couldn't stay long—I had to get home and get suited up.

'Are you best man, at least?' Grandma said.

'That'll be Nifty's brother, Tristan. Remember Nifty?'

Dad switched the TV back on and she turned to it, absorbed instantly by *A Place in the Sun* or whatever it was. Soon we were back outside, sucking in lungfuls of odourless air. An hour later, The Shark picked me up in his deep green soft-top Audi.

'Look at this trendy weapon,' he said.

My red gingham tie was brand new, the most expensive I'd ever bought. My charcoal suit, tailored specially, cost more than all my other suits combined. My brogues were polished to excess, gleaming like little seals.

'Fashion,' I said. 'You should try it sometime.'

We screeched away and careened across the island with roof down and music booming. His girlfriend Tara was crammed into the back, holding her blonde hair in place. The car had earned him some stick over the years but on a day like that it was hard to fault. At my request, we took the scenic route, down to Pleinmont and up the west coast, swooping around the bays. Portelet, Vazon, Cobo, Grandes Rocques, all glittering and strewn with children, towels, parasols. Tyres squealing, we cornered into Port Soif. The stacks of rock that flank the bay stood basking in the sun. One, the furthest out, towered above the others. The Wells. The mere sight of it filled me with dread.

Scrawny kids, we had huddled up there, on windy low-tide afternoons when no one was around, blustering about the day when we would make the leap. We knew the Wells was compulsory, knew what happened to the reputations of those who chose to climb down, shaking and pale, rather than jump. I asked my grandfather once where the name came from. As far as he knew, he said, it was named for the first lad to jump it, who had broken his spine and never walked again. No way, I told him, you're just trying to put me off.

There was a ledge where a few could sit, below and to the side of the pinnacle, usually reserved for jumpers. There was space behind for six or so more—from there you got the atmosphere but saw only departures, not landings. Most people watched from a lower stand of rocks on the other side of the horseshoe bay. Even to spectate was dizzying for me, to bellow the countdown then count the seconds as a body dropped, to roar with the crowd as it resurfaced, arms aloft. Broken legs happened at least once a summer, windings and cracked ribs almost weekly. It was another world, an arena where classroom hierarchies meant nothing. Beaucamps, St Sampson's, Grammar, Elizabeth College—your school, your grades, your skills on the pitch meant nothing compared to how you handled your moment on the Wells.

The Shark must have noticed me gazing out there. 'Should've done it, Scarfy,' he shouted across. 'Should've fucking done it.'

Each summer growing up we had mastered one of the lesser jumps—Havelet, Albecq, the Vazon wall— moving steadily closer to the ultimate. It wasn't until that last summer, Penny's summer, that our turn finally came. Nifty had a tide table, and the day, the hour, was circled with a red felt-tip pen. 4.30 p.m., Tuesday, 12 August 1997. Every night for a week I shouted myself awake, clutching the shin or ankle I'd shattered in a dream. Even the smaller jumps had been a struggle for me, and I knew with absolute certainty I couldn't do the Wells. It would be one thing to fail in front of my friends, but in front of her?

Since that day at Petit Port, I'd made no real progress, though she'd held my hand a few times walking through town, always letting go after less than a minute. And when we all piled into Nifty's car, it was my lap she sat on. Don't let her mess you about, the boys said. But anything was better than being ignored. In the end, I faked a stomach bug two days before. I knew they didn't believe me, but they were decent enough to pretend next time we all met up. Penny didn't mention it either, her silence the one that bothered me most. Worst of all, it turned out that she had jumped too—one of only four girls ever, apparently.

I wasn't there to see it. But I can picture her up there even now.

'Would you do it again?' I yelled back at The Shark. He was drumming with some vigour on the steering wheel.

'Not a chance, mate. It's like garden running, or nicking booze. You have to be young. Young and stupid. Invincible. Nothing to lose.' He turned off the coast road and swung into the car park behind the church. 'If you took me up there now, I'd bawl and blow chunks.'

Tara leaned between us to turn down the music and kiss him on the cheek. 'I know,' he said, 'I know.' He climbed out and tilted the seat for her. I found myself unable to move. Somewhere in that church, Penny was waiting. I would walk in, collect my order of service and my pouch of confetti, and from somewhere in the crowd she would turn and wave and lavish me with that smile.

'Come on, then,' The Shark said, pointing at me with his keys. 'I didn't get all dressed up to stand in the bloody car park.'

A few days after they'd all jumped, Penny and Alexis had left for Biarritz with the Newtons. I spent the fortnight they were gone developing an elaborate plan for telling her how I felt, a plan that included sixty-two tealights, one for each day since we'd met. But when they came back—it was the Monday after Diana died in Paris—she was different. No arm around my waist when we stood in the pub, no head on my shoulder by the fire on the beach, no absent-minded stroking of the fingertip scar that had earned me my nickname. On her last night, we all went out, drinking harder than we had all summer, and wound up in a circle on the dancefloor in Folies, Penny in the middle. I remember the blissed-out look on her face as she danced. The lights all seemed to be pointing at her.

Afterwards, out in the predawn street, Alexis yelling 'Quick!' from inside a waiting cab, she hugged everyone, kissing cheeks, telling us how much she loved us all, how she'd definitely be back. By then I was one in a line of devotees, dutifully waiting my turn.

But then, to my astonishment, she kissed me on the mouth. Five, ten seconds—a real kiss. Stunned, I watched as she dug a biro out of her handbag and scrawled her address on my left palm. *Clayton Manor, near Tetbury, Glocs.* Even I knew what kind of house that meant. Before I could say a word, she had climbed into the cab, which sped off, leaving me standing there, beaming.

'Bye, Posh Penny,' someone said.

At first, we rarely wrote more than twice a year. The urge to respond at once was always strong, but I had to resist. It seemed important to let enough time pass for interesting things to occur. Her letters were thrilling, headlong rushes, and the prospect of boring her with mine was appalling. No one else from home was in touch with her, even Alexis only vaguely—Penny didn't use a mobile, said she hated email. When Facebook appeared, I searched for her, knowing it was pointless. Those letters were all I had. Each time, after the second and third months of waiting, I would sullenly accept that I had faded from her thoughts. But then an envelope would appear, some kind of ornate doodle on the back, and I'd be smitten all over again.

Do you keep my letters, Ned? We were both about to graduate, me from Aberdeen, she from Corpus Christi. *I hope so. I feel as though one day I'd like to read them all again. Everything is a blur, the last few years have absolutely disappeared.*

They were, I suppose, an addiction—a series of intermittent fixes, breaking up my unremarkable life. When one bland morning or week or month could be transformed by the arrival of something amazing—something to prove I was still on the mind of a girl never far from mine—what chance did every other morning stand? Every other week or month?

I went back to Guernsey, broke. Eventually I took a job at an estate agency. Dad and me in the old house, moping, getting on each other's nerves. Meanwhile, Penny was roaming the globe, volunteering in orphanages, on sustainable farms, teaching English to refugees. Each letter seemed sent from a different continent, battered by its voyage. There was always some escapade, some crisis of her own making, more amusing than concerning to her, though I often found myself holding my breath as I read. *Why do I do these things? Who knows, but at least once I do them, they're done.* To the rare ones that included a return address, I replied as fast as I could, abandoning all pride in the hope of catching her before she moved on. From Guate-mala, a postcard—*What a palaver!* From Bangladesh, a feverish note—*They hate me, I can tell, they blame me for the harvest, the dead baby, everything, I'm too sick to care* . . . By then I was twenty-four. My brother finished his degree, came home for three months and moved to London. I decided to do the same. Not that I was following him—it was more, if you don't go now, you never will. Tom felt worse about leaving Dad alone than I did, but he hadn't spent the past two years living with him.

Around that time, Penny took herself back to Kenya. Her letters were still infrequent, but longer than ever. She devoted pages to the details of her life, the land-scape, the people she met. *Maybe it's because I was here before, but the moment I arrived I felt exactly that—I had arrived. I was home! I've never quite felt that until now.* She wrote about the skies. She said she could feel the world revealing itself like nowhere else. *You must come. You must see it.*

I could have gone, of course. I had money for a ticket. But I was afraid of disproving the version of myself I'd presented in my letters. Hers was a life that towered over mine—I was still the boy who stayed at home when everybody jumped. Better to keep writing, I thought. The day will come.

Two hundred-plus people filled the church. Spotting Penny was impossible, but it was enough to know she was somewhere in the crowd. In her last letter, a couple of months ago, she'd sounded excited about the wed-ding. *Finally, back to little Guernsey!* Up at the front, Nifty was waving to people, pulling terrified faces, lunging and stretching in preparation. He looked less nervous than I felt.

The ceremony was long, but I willed it to go on, to delay the moment we would gather outside and at last stand face to face. But I didn't see her outside either. There were people to catch up with, hands to shake. The photographer got up on a stepladder and herded us about—she wanted a picture of the whole crowd. She kept calling Nifty by his real name, Howard. A cheer went up every time.

There were coaches to the reception at the Gables Hotel, an old place behind the airport. Someone produced a hipflask and passed it around. Obscene songs were soon being sung. Some older guests and girlfriends looked unimpressed but the boys were beyond reproach— it was Nifty's big day and, by extension, theirs. I tried to join in, but my chest felt tight, I couldn't get enough air in to sing. By the time we reached the hotel the flask was empty and The Shark had made Tara cry.

In the bar, I glanced over people's shoulders, scanning the sea of faces. Could she have changed so much that I didn't recognize her? I pushed my way over to the seating plan. My own name jumped out easily enough but not the one I wanted to see. Back and forth across the lists I went until no doubt remained.

As we filed into dinner past Nifty and Alexis, I restrained myself from asking. In a haze of disappointment, I struggled through the meal, prodding at the bass on my plate—I'd picked it remembering that day at Petit

Port, imagining Penny doing the same. Instead she hadn't even shown up. Typical Penny, I thought, trying to feel more cross than upset. The Shark kept filling and refilling my glass, flirting with the youngest De Lisle girl, Tara beside him looking glum. Tristan's speech had everyone in stitches, but I barely heard a word.

Soon enough the music was starting, the tables cleared away, the first game couples taking to the floor. Sandy De Lisle, Alexis's mum, went straight for Nifty, which provoked another cheer. I found myself standing alone, not far from the bar. Tristan came over, slapped me on the back and handed me a pint. His black hair was thinner than last time I saw him, with grey flecks by the ears. His face was fuller too. We talked about his speech, his own wedding out in Sydney, where he'd been living the past few years.

After a while I said, 'You remember Alexis's friend Penny?'

He turned to me with the strangest expression. He blew out his cheeks, shook his head. 'Horrific, eh?'

My heart skipped.

'Horrific. Can't say we ever kept in touch, but I never forgot her, that's for sure. Quite a girl.' He gazed off across the room. 'That trip to Biarritz.' There was a faint smile on his lips. 'Mum and Dad put the girls in one room, me and Nift in the other. Well, you can imagine how long that lasted. He sneaked off down the hall and there was Penny tiptoeing through the door, all apologetic. Said goodnight and went to sleep. Every night for two weeks. Drove me insane! I was what, nineteen?

Twenty? Absolutely insane. Then on the last night we all got hammered at dinner and went out and when she came in that time she had a sheet wrapped around her. A sheet and nothing else. Let it drop, climbed in. Unbelievable. And then never spoke to me again. Not a *word*, I mean.' He shook his head. 'Quite a girl.'

He carried on, waving his hands, oblivious to the blows he was landing. 'Lex was really cut up, talking about postponing. But we said that's the last thing Penny would've wanted.'

He looked at me then. I saw his eyes widen. 'Oh, shit, Ned. Didn't you know?'

I swallowed, shrugged. I tried to say *Know what?* but nothing came.

'Ned, she died. Like five days ago. Some kind of accident in Ghana or Kenya or somewhere.'

'Kenya,' I managed to say. It seemed important. Of course, it could have been anywhere.

'Kenya, yeah.' He paused. 'Had you kept in touch, then?'

I might have nodded.

'I think it was a bus crash, but I'm not one hundred per cent. You'd have to ask Nift.' He put his hand on my shoulder. 'Maybe not tonight, though, eh?'

His pregnant, blonde, Australian wife appeared and dragged him on to the dancefloor. I stood alone at the edge. Through the crowd I caught a glimpse of Nifty and Alexis, spinning in the blinking lights. Maybe it was their clothes, but suddenly they seemed like strangers. They'd known as well as anyone how I felt about Penny that summer. I never told them about the letters, and Alexis had never mentioned them to me, which implied that Penny had kept our secret. Or maybe it had just never meant as much to her as it had to me.

The music faded as I walked. The night was clear and warm. The airport was closed, the field still, the dark hulks of planes like sleeping animals. I followed the road that marked the perimeter and then on through the fragrant lanes heading west. There were hedgehogs, bats, a sleek black cat that rubbed against my calves, then dashed away. I don't know how long it took—an hour or two, probably. I know the moon was bright enough to cast my shadow out in front of me. And I remember reciting lines from her letters, lines I hadn't known I'd memorized but which returned fully formed as I walked.

I looked it up that evening, back in my London room. Tristan was right—a bus crash. She'd been riding on the roof with the bags and some tourists when it veered into a ditch. Apparently, she was thrown some distance, broke her neck on impact, died instantly. Now there was an image in my head I couldn't shake. Mid-air, caught in the sunlight as if in amber. Two others were killed, the article said, Belgians.

At least once I do them, they're done.

It was still dark when I reached Port Soif. I picked my way down the dunes through the sturdy grass and sat in my suit on the cool sand. A faint swell was ambling into the bay. My eyes had adjusted to the light by then, but everything still seemed unreal.

I don't know how long I sat there. I thought about my

life, what it had been so far and what it might still become. Tints of daybreak leaked into the sky as one gull after another began to squawk. I could feel the air getting chillier. The Wells loomed all the while at the edge of the bay, and I watched it, waiting for something. A sign.

When it came, I told myself, whatever it was, I would stand and make my way out to the first low section of exposed reef. I would climb steadily, the rock face cool under my hands, the old cracks and footholds where they always were. At the top, I would stand looking out at the water, behind me the beach, coast road, houses, everything perfectly quiet. I would sway in the breeze, the infamous breeze, I would sway but be unafraid. The fear of slipping, the infamous fear, I would be beyond it. I would button my jacket, straighten my tie, move my left foot up to the edge, grip the rock through the leather soles of my brogues. I'd look down, way down to where I needed to hit. Eleven years late, but still I would hear them, calling my name and howling like children, counting me down from five to one.

4. You Must, You Will

Flora and Jonathan were reading in bed when he made the announcement. Two evenings a week, until further notice, he would be running home from the office. She laughed once, curtly, like spitting.

'That's really,' she said, 'really quite far. Why not work up to it? We could go around the park on Saturday.'

He pointed out that she ran only on weekdays, preferring to avoid 'weekend wobblers'. Surprised by how mean this phrase of hers sounded, she shook two multivitamins out, swallowed one and, indulging a habit that would prove tenacious even long after he was gone, held the other out for him to take.

'I wouldn't mind *together*,' she said. Tablet glow lit her face, scrubbed clean of make-up and doused with lotion. Reading glasses perched on her long nose—she only wore them around the house. On her nightstand lay a hand-tooled notebook for the recording of important nocturnal thoughts. The most recent entry—*Celeriac?*—was several weeks old.

He wasn't looking for a personal trainer, he said, just telling her not to expect him, supper-wise, much before nine. He leafed through the latest *Monocle*. His pyjamas, patterned with tiny bicycles though it was twenty-plus years since he'd ridden one, had been purchased and wrapped by Flora as a gift from their eldest daughter, Annabel.

'Supper-wise,' she said, pleased at least by the sound of the word. In the thriller she was reading, a man in a woolly hat had just cut out a woman's tongue. Now Flora's tongue felt enormous in her mouth, enormous and wonderful. 'New voice on your phone today?'

She'd called around eleven to pass on the news of their middle child's third detention this term, as reported in an email from the head. Since Sally had never been any trouble before she went off to Millfield, and since Flora had begged Jonathan not to send her away—for the girl's own good, supposedly, though in truth her motives were more selfish than that—she was really calling for vindication. The new PA—Melissa was her name—had seemed talkative and incompetent, promising so emphatically to pass on the message that Flora had been sure she'd forget.

In the end, they'd had the detention chat getting into bed, Jonathan receiving the news with a smirk. Flora looked across to see him staring at a perfume ad, bringing the page to his nose for a sniff. She could smell his last cigarette of the day. His hair seemed greyer than the last time she'd looked—how unfair that it only improved a man. Her own would need doing soon, not that he'd notice unless she shaved it all off or coloured it pink like that Spanish girl at Nero. Imagine. The look on his face.

She ran first thing, empty stomach, any weather, for the purity, the monastic rhythm—so she told other mothers when they said they'd seen her in the park. In fact, she rarely braved the rain. With Jonathan gone before she even woke up, she lingered with Charlie in the kitchen, watching his cartoons, wolfing sugary fistfuls of his preferred cereal straight from the box. He had a way of looking at her, half accusing and half amused, silver eyes narrowed, smiling with the left side of his mouth. Our secret, she told him, though even the boy didn't know that once he left for school she poured a deep bowlful for herself. So kind of you to share, she told him. Those early minutes were the day's best, Charlie's orange curls still flat from his pillow, and she knew that when Jonathan tried to send him away too, she would fight like a lioness to keep him home.

Once the Frosties had been eaten, she had no choice but to run. The artificial sweetness, fuzzy tongue and aching teeth, the delicious surge of guilt propelled her out into the street.

She ran without music, O-shaped water flask gripped in fist. Her shoes, so comfortable that to remove them was unpleasant, had cost nearly two hundred pounds. According to the treadmill at Runners Need, they were perfectly suited to the way she landed—heavily on the heel's outside edge. She wore them for days at a time, to the bakery, the deli, the fishmonger's, even to Nero with Zoe.

'This morning,' Zoe said, flawless in black leather jacket and heeled knee-high boots, 'I stood in front of the mirror and thought, who are you even dressing up for?'

But then Flora watched as the good-looking young

waiter gave her friend a *pain au chocolat* on the house—the pink-haired girl looked sullenly on—and as outside a white van executed an emergency stop so Zoe could cross the road. Flora watched the three men in the van watch her friend, then went home and called the salon. Later, ashamed by the shoes but unwilling to change, she cancelled the appointment with minutes to spare.

She ran alone, trying to land more lightly on her heels, hearing the air pile into her lungs and billow out again, hearing the metronomic thud of her pulse. Along the Fulham Road, past the bookshop and the cinema, down to the river, where the light changed and the sky opened up, over Battersea Bridge past stationary buses with glum faces turned to the windows, east into the park, dewy grass and glistening leaves. She ran laps, past the lake and tennis courts, past the Peace Pagoda which every woman in Chelsea *just loved*.

Zoe was so funny about that.

Two laps was four miles, and by now she felt it in her knees and hips, not fatigue or pain so much as what their Pilates teacher called the limitations of her body. Honour, the teacher said, feet behind head. Honour and disobey.

The city had always looked best when she was moving. She'd never forgotten the train ride down from Durham, after graduation in 1993—the way it all finally rose up at the window, like men pushing back their chairs to stand as she came into a room. A guy across the aisle had chatted her up, said he worked at Radio 4. She'd wanted so badly to believe him. Soon she was doing publicity at one of the big houses, pouring wine at launches, sending out bound proofs. She kept a toothbrush and a fresh pair of knickers at the office for the nights she didn't make it home. Jonathan she met in the spring—his PR agency had the Booker contract. The third time they spoke, he asked if she was seeing anyone. That he checked was disappointing, and she said yes to test him. He was seven years older—the perfect gap, she thought.

They married within a year, in Guernsey at Torteval parish church, close to her parents' house. A tussle broke out at the reception, and one of her cousins was dragged outside, chin slick with blood. When Annabel was born in the autumn, the girls from work sent flowers—*We miss you! Come back ASAP!* Sweet of them to say, Jonathan said. Nothing came, though, when Sally or Charlie arrived. Most of them were having children of their own by then, but she couldn't help picturing them all squeezed around a table at The Fox & Goose, sinking pints and filling ashtrays, cackling.

For her thirtieth birthday, he took her to Paris, her first time on the Eurostar. Only when the train plunged into the darkness did she realize she'd imagined a clear, aquarium-style tunnel. The disappointment was terrible, though what had she possibly expected to see? She kept it to herself. Later, at a noisy Montmartre bistro, waited on by a girl so effortlessly stunning she was like a blade cutting through the smoke, Flora drank too much wine and missed the children so badly she could hardly eat. At the hotel, she fell asleep, still in her blue dress and shoes,

Jonathan out on the balcony smoking, calling the view tremendous.

Every summer since Charlie was born, she had taken all three of them to Guernsey for a fortnight. Her parents' house had only three bedrooms, so there were fold-out cots wherever you looked. Jonathan joined them reluctantly for a long weekend in the middle, blaming the briefness on work. Last year, after eight straight days of rain, Annabel had declared that she wouldn't be going again. She wanted to go away with her friends, to their family villas in Tuscany and Mallorca, no doubt to sneak out into the Continental night and be kissed and touched by beautiful, dark-haired boys. Flora knew she should understand. Besides, at fifteen the girl grew less and less pleasant to be around. But it had always seemed important that her children know and love the island of her own youth, even if the place had felt suffocating to her by the time she'd reached that age herself. She couldn't help equating their loss of interest in the island with a loss of interest in her. She wanted them to know the world beyond their capsule of privilege, or at least to know that free things were valuable too. Cliff walks over Petit Bôt, crabbing at Portelet, camping in Herm—some things she remembered more clearly than others, but even the parts she never thought of at all were in her somewhere, doing their work, like vitamins, like a breath.

'Trying to impress her?' Zoe said. 'Or something more sinister?'

Flora cut her pastry into four equal parts and put one

in her mouth. Outside the café window, February rain came down. 'He staggers in, head-to-toe running gear, gasping, straight into the shower. Eats whatever I put in front of him, glass and a half of red, cigarette and into bed. I've never known him fall asleep so fast.'

Zoe shook her head. 'I told Brian on our honeymoon that if he ever cheated on me, I'd cut off his dick with a steak knife. It helped that I had it in my hand at the time.'

'The knife?'

'Last night he told me apropos of literally nothing that his high-school sweetheart used to swallow.'

Zoe had met Brian at Syracuse. He'd wound up at Goldman's, and after the crash had been transferred over the pond, their son Jude soon appearing in Charlie's class. Seven years younger than Flora, Zoe had made no friends and complained frequently about Chelsea women. 'You wouldn't believe how that snooty bitch looked at me . . .' Sometimes she developed elaborate schemes to get back at whoever had pissed her off—inviting them over for brunch, say, then cancelling, rescheduling, cancelling again. Flora, who had told Jonathan many times that she wished they'd never left Clapham, understood. She was fond of the American to an extent that made her nervous, in the same way that as a schoolgirl she'd been reluctant to designate a best friend without first being selected herself. She'd read somewhere that an only child will often struggle to make people laugh. Knowing this had suddenly seemed to make it true.

'Not your style?' she said, chewing.

Zoe gave her a look. 'Oh, we have a system. Bri taps

me on the shoulder at the last second and I dive out of the way.'

Flora nodded. 'I never minded, personally.'

Zoe loved that.

After coffee they went into the bookshop. Isaac, behind the counter, knew her name and waved—apologetically, she always thought.

'Anything new and spectacular?' she would say, at least once a week. She never left without a hardback biography, an obscure translated novel, some poetry. These went unread on to the dining-room shelves— she'd get to them one day, or not. Her trick was to covertly browse the thrillers, photographing one or two with her phone for downloading later on the tablet. Isaac hated tablets and she never mentioned hers, instead telling him stories of her working days—riding in a taxi with Amis and Hitchens, booking flights for Barnes. About himself, Isaac gave little away. He was twenty-eight or so, she guessed, a frustrated poet, sharing a poky Streatham flat with an old friend. That day he sold Flora a coffee-table book of war photography. 'Oh, Bill Pointer,' she said. The name was vaguely familiar. 'Yes, of course.'

'You should seduce him,' Zoe said, back outside. 'Show the poor kid the ropes.'

For a moment, Flora was stunned by the image—on her knees behind the counter, sweaty in her running shoes, customers browsing obliviously as Isaac poured himself into her mouth. She blinked it away, shifted the heavy book bag from one shoulder to another.

'I just love it when you blush,' Zoe said, touching Flora's cheek.

She had a long-held belief that she was hard to embarrass. Unflappable. When she was seventeen, the big joke at Ladies' College had been inspired by her namesake margarine and a rumour no one would confess to starting. *Flora spreads easily.* The teasing hadn't bothered her—in fact she had relished the status it conferred. 1989, year of the drought. Early in the summer, a young family had moved in next door. Along with his rust-brown lawn and dead hydrangeas, her father had moaned daily about the noise the two boys made playing out in the long, warm evenings.

She'd been seeing a scaffolder called Natty, mostly because other girls were doing something similar and it had become a sort of unacknowledged slumming competition. Meredith—everyone called her Fauna—had recently lost her virginity to a bricklayer with *Satan My Saviour* tattooed calligraphically across his shoulders, describing the experience as 'lush'. Natty was tattoo-free but drove a lowered Golf GTI with booming speakers in the back. He called her Floz or, sometimes, Flozzie.

She'd spoken to Roger, the new man next door, once or twice over the fence. He seemed afraid of her, something Natty definitely wasn't, and she found herself thinking of him at odd times. While showering, for example, or clipping her nails. He had a nervous, effeminate way of fussing with his hair when he talked. Once, clearing up after a barbecue, she'd heard the wife shouting hysterically, his only response a series of sullen mumblings.

One weekend in early September, her parents went to Saint-Malo. I've asked Roger to keep an eye on you, her mother said, his wife's away too so he's got his hands full, don't bother him unless you have to. She didn't tell Natty the house was empty—there'd been some disastrous parties—so that night he drove her out to the moorings at Saint's. She watched him pour Smirnoff into a half-empty Coke and smoke a B&H while she drank it. His hair was buzzed so short on the sides she could see his pale scalp. He pulled her over, kissed her briefly, pushed her head down. Roger appeared again in her mind, paint-brush adorably in hand, cowering like a puppy on his roof that morning as the Red Arrows had roared over-head. She pushed back hard against Natty's hand, sat up and asked to be taken home.

Back on Jerbourg Road, as the Golf sped away and she fumbled tearfully for her keys, she saw Roger through his living-room window, alone on the sofa. His long hair, even wilder than usual, seemed to have paint in it. He looked boyish, sitting hands and knees together like that. In need of reassurance. She clattered up the driveway to knock on the door.

When at last he opened up, the telephone was ringing. His eyes were wide as he ushered her in and went into the kitchen to answer the call. Alone in the living room, she looked around, tipsy on the vodka but composed. That morning, sunbathing in the garden, she'd caught him watching her from up on his roof as he painted the chimney or whatever he was doing. Now she saw white paint all over the carpet, thickest on the granite slabs where the fireplace should have been. The fumes were dizzying—had he dropped the pot down the chimney or something? Half-empty boxes were strewn around, furniture carelessly arranged. She could hear him on the phone but not what he said. The house was structurally like hers but shabbier, worse. She went into the little bathroom by the back door. In the mirror she saw that her mascara had run.

She found him standing as if lost in his own living room. 'Hello, mister neighbour.'

He turned. 'Flora, are you all right?'

Everything felt cosy and innocent. Outside the sky was losing light, the day's heat fading. She put her arms around him and after a moment he did the same. Neither let go and then he was inhaling the smell of her hair and touching his lips to her forehead. She felt him grow hard against her hip and even that was endearing, nothing like with Natty. She pressed herself against him, turned her mouth up to his.

He tasted like salt and vinegar, like chip-shop chips. Also a bit of wine. Her tongue felt bigger than his, though surely it couldn't be. After a while, she pushed him gently back on to the sofa. His hands lay flat, palms down against the cushion, as if he were steadying himself. As she knelt, thinking before she even began that she would never be able to tell anyone about this, footsteps sounded through the ceiling.

Roger leaped up instantly, bumping her forehead with

his hip. He led her, almost dragged her, towards the front door. As he opened it, though they didn't meet hers, she saw fear in his eyes. Before it closed behind her, she heard a child's voice at the top of the stairs say, 'Daddy? Are you there?'

Then she was in her own house, in a better-decorated replica of the hallway from which she'd just been expelled, expecting to cry but grinning instead, spinning like a dancer to the fridge for some milk.

'You must have seen him all the time,' Zoe said. They were in her kitchen, mid-afternoon, leaning against the polished granite worktops, drinking Sauvignon blanc. Radio 4 was on, a man's voice declaring that the protests in Tahrir Square left Egypt's prime minister with no option but to resign.

'We moved later that year, thank God. But I did see him a few years back, on the beach. He looked so old. Must be nearly sixty now.'

'You spoke?'

'Christ, no. I was with the kids. He recognized me, though, I'm sure. He looked at Annabel like she was a ghost.'

'Is this what you wanted to tell me? Because we've all made our married-man-mistakes.'

Flora shook her head.

'Uh oh.'

Zoe refilled their glasses.

'Last night, I ran out of garlic,' Flora said, 'right at the crucial moment. Dashed out to Sainsbury's and what do

I see? Jonny. Getting out of a cab in his running gear and jogging off up Beaufort Street with his pathetic little backpack.'

Zoe's eyes were fascinated. 'He sees you?'

Another headshake. 'Next thing I know I'm flagging down the cab, saying fifty quid to go once round the block if you tell me where you picked my husband up and exactly what he said. He thinks about it—these bastards—but when I show him the cash he says, "Crouch End. Said name any great man in history, they all had at least one mistress." Apparently his examples were Napoleon, JFK and some old Brazilian footballer.'

'Napoleon? Are you kidding me?'

Flora shrugged. 'This morning I call his office and have a nice little chat with this Melissa. Guess where she tells me she lives?'

Zoe threw her arms up, spilled her wine. Flora watched her wipe off the worktop, the white tiles. Then her friend went quiet for a while, and Flora could see she was having one of her ideas.

It took a few days and dozens of calls each. With only ten weeks to go, all places had long been filled, but Zoe was sure there had to be a charity willing to bend the rules for the right price.

A woman called Victoria proved to be the one. She had a girl at Millfield too, and had been to Guernsey once for the Battle of Flowers. Pleasant enough, she said, if you like that sort of thing. Victoria represented Cancel Cancer, whose runners had to raise at least five thousand each. No, she had no objection to a direct donation. None whatsoever.

'When do I tell him?' Flora asked later at Pilates. They were stretched out on purple mats, surrounded by limbs and grimaces.

'Oh, not for a while,' Zoe said. The pleasure of plotting was all over her face. 'We don't actually want him getting in shape, right?'

'I suppose not.'

In her thrillers, it was always a girl being murdered or mutilated by a man. The formula should have got boring, but it never did. Still, she'd often thought, why not switch it around? Months later, after the funeral, when the condolence cards had been stuffed in a drawer, when Zoe and Brian had moved back to the States (to Westchester, to work on their marriage, whatever that meant) and Charlie had passed the Millfield entrance exam, she would remember this moment—how her hamstrings felt tight, how the teacher looked exhausted. She would wonder how differently things might have turned out if she'd never met Zoe at all.

She bought a new pair of the same shoes and a special watch that monitored her heart rate. When Isaac said he was sure she'd do fine, she detected him glancing down at her body, assessing her machinery. From him she bought books on marathon training that she hid under the bed, consulting them only when alone. On her tablet she bought apps to track her progress, plot her routes.

She ran laps of the park, one more each time. She ran the river, all the way to Greenwich and back or out to

Richmond or Wimbledon, in miserable drizzle or perfect blue stillness, further every week. On the South Bank, she weaved through dawdling tourists, imagining how she must look to them—woman of the city, solitary, adamant, unconstrained by timetables and maps. At Canary Wharf, towers swaying overhead, she heard in her mind the spectacular noise of the hordes who would gather on race day, cheers ringing out down the glassy canyons. London itself re-emerged as she ran, parading and presenting itself as it had when she'd first arrived, almost twenty years ago now, dragging two suitcases up the King's Cross escalators. You can do this, she told herself, a word for each stride, over and over, you can do this, you must, you will.

Honour and disobey, Zoe said.

Finally, with six weeks to go, she told him. He was in his robe, fresh out of the shower, eating curry she had made from scratch. He froze, loaded fork hanging. She sat opposite, thighs throbbing from that morning's nine miles, watching the twitch of panic.

'Us?' he said. 'Did you say *entered us?*'

She smiled. 'I'm so proud of you.' The words that Zoe had scripted for her fell a little woodenly out of her mouth. 'All this running! You're so much happier, so energetic. You're –' She faltered. 'You're like a new man.'

He stared at her, then down at his plate. She could see it seeping in. His jaw swelled by his ears as he ground his teeth.

'Do you know what yesterday was?' she said, off script now. She saw his eyes widen. 'Sixteen years. All

I want'—he tried to interrupt, but she raised a hand and went on—'all I want is to do this together. No jewellery, no restaurant, no fucking *perfume*. This.'

Upstairs, Charlie yelled in triumph at a video game. Before Jonathan could answer, she reached across, hand a little shaky, picked up his glass of red and went, sipping, to tell her son to get ready for bed.

Greenwich Park teemed with people. Eight in the morning, grey cloud, fine drizzle settling in. Under a yellow awning they congregated with other Cancel Cancer runners, everyone stretching, pacing on the spot, chattering nervously. She tied and retied her shoelaces, Jonathan pale and silent nearby. They had run together only a handful of times, he gasping and limping beside her. Earlier that week, after running home from work—apparently determined, despite it all, to maintain that particular pretence—he'd paused as he struggled up the stairs, one hand gripping the banister, the other at his throat. She'd watched him from the sofa, the big book of harrowing photographs she'd bought from Isaac open on her lap, willing him to call to her so she could go to him.

They joined the stream of runners approaching the start. Many wore flimsy clear ponchos for the rain. Jonathan said, 'We don't have ponchos *why*?'

People all around them wished each other luck. Several were in costume—nurses, vampires, Supermen, some wearing shoes like hers. Music pounded from speakers draped with plastic sheeting, while, at the railings, spectators cheered and clapped. Zoe would be on The Mall with Jude and Charlie later to watch them enter the home straight. But all that was more than four hours off.

They passed under the gate and everyone began to run. Excitement flooded her limbs—she could go for fifty miles, a hundred, more.

'*For Christ's sake slow down*,' Jonathan hissed.

After the first heady rush, they fell into a rhythm. They were out on the south-eastern edge of the city—Woolwich, Charlton, Westcombe Park—bleak residential tracts she had never seen. The crowd out there was thin, locals strung along the rain-soaked pavements giving desultory yelps of support. She'd been warned to expect this of the first half. Later the noise would be incredible, along the Embankment with the end in sight, all those miles behind her, the raucous stands strewn with banners and flags.

They ran side by side in marital silence, passing or being passed. Every thirty seconds, he hawked and spat. She heard his breathing over her own, glimpsed the pain on his face. The giddiness had faded, but still she felt strong, no more strained than if she were walking. The rain came down harder, relentless and cool.

They passed the six-mile marker after seventy-five minutes, back at Greenwich Park, heading west along the northern edge, less than a mile from where they began. Six of twenty-six. She felt his mood darken.

After Sally had arrived, when Flora had been trapped at home all day with a baby and a toddler, Jonathan's agency had merged with another. He worked all hours, travelled most weeks. Adrift in those housebound afternoons, she wondered where her life had gone—nights in The Fox, endless parties, the sense of being exactly where she belonged. This was in Clapham, before the move across the river. She'd grown convinced he was having an affair, something he denied again and again—you're losing it, he told her, you're stewing in these silly ideas. Later, she realized the girl she'd pictured was a teenaged version of herself, the room littered with boxes and spilled white paint. She wondered now whether by accusing him and staying she had given him a kind of permission.

Fuck *that*, Zoe would say.

Twenty-six miles. It occurred to her, suddenly, that that was as long as the coastline of Guernsey. Nine miles up, five across, twenty-six around—numbers she would never forget. But her island felt like another world now. And could she really call it hers any more? She had left it behind, that was the truth. Best thing she ever did.

He wheezed now, arms limp, shoes scuffing the tarmac. 'Go on if you want,' he said. She shook her head, but she wanted to run faster, to surge ahead into the wide Westminster streets, the roar of the waiting crowds, Zoe's face there among all the others.

'Yes,' he said, panting, nodding. 'Go, go.'

She jogged at his side, low houses reeling past, knowing she should say something. Instead she reached out and squeezed his hand until she felt him squeeze back. Then she let go and she was driving with her arms, kicking up her legs, faster and faster until she was sprinting, the space between them opening up. She was passing people half and twice her age, girls in tiny skin-tight shorts, hairy-shouldered men, two walking bearded angels who soon enough would be kneeling over him there on the tarmac, plastic wings flapping as they pounded on his chest and tried to pass air from their lungs into his.

5. Fear the Greeks

Athens at six in the August evening was loud and shrouded by fumes. At last, Tom found them a room near Omónia, mattress sweat-stained and rife with bugs. On the floor was a brimming glass ashtray. To divert her attention away from the squalor, he asked Becca if she was hungry. With her back to him, she stood at the open window in jeans and a yellow vest, tan telling the story of her jobless summer, dark hair longer than he'd expected to find it. There were unfamiliar mannerisms too.

'Say what, now?' she said—this, for instance.

The coming weeks seemed a desert they must cross together, a desert not unlike the one Heracles had faced, deep in the tenth of his twelve labours, firing impotent arrows at the sun. That morning, delayed in the airless Gatwick lounge, he'd waited for her to say that she didn't want to go, they shouldn't be going, something was wrong. Instead she'd been almost giddy. She stood, checked the screen, sat down, stood again. Finally, he'd cleared his throat and announced that the whole trip would be his treat. 'As in, I've got it covered. It's on me.' Don't be ridiculous, she'd said. But he'd insisted. 'My gift to you.' Imitating some other man, wealthier, more assured. 'You deserve it.'

At that, she'd failed to suppress a smile.

No, she said now, she wasn't hungry, maybe they should just go to sleep. Despite the heat, she wouldn't undress, blaming the multitudinous bugs. In bed together for the first time in weeks, they lay parallel, sweating.

As she slept, he opened the guidebook, read again about the Parthenon. The facts were agreeably familiar—9:4 ratio, illusory curves, imperceptible slant of columns, harmony of design. The temple had fascinated him since he'd first encountered it in a child's encyclopaedia, aged seven. As a boy, he'd been inclined to play alone, his quiet pursuits mocked by his athletic elder brother. He'd concocted and enacted perilous missions, leading invented armies, defeating imaginary enemies, aligning with the classical heroes and their plights—Theseus v. Minotaur, Odysseus v. Cyclops. Later he'd learned that these fixations could pass as scholarly interests. At fifteen, thanks to an appendectomy the night before departure, he'd missed the school trip to Greece. Three years later, he'd been one of the only Ancient History freshers at Leeds never to have made the fabled climb up to the Acropolis.

He dozed off, book on chest, and dreamed of reaching the Beulé Gate, arriving at last in glorious sunlight, struck dumb by the splendour, comfortable in sandals. When his alarm rang in the morning, she was already in the shower.

They walked around the Pláka, jostling with tourists in bright white trainers and many-pocketed shorts. He caught himself searching for things to say, ways to make her laugh. He felt as nervous as he had on the night they'd met, watching a band called Fear the Greeks in a smoky room above a Leeds pub. The date was carved into his memory—13 January 2002. After the set, he'd wound up at the far end of a long, narrow table, at which ten or twelve people he barely knew had sat. Next to him was Becca. Her friend Lindsay was sleeping with the singer, she said. Oh, really? he said, though he already knew. Their isolation from the group was unnerving, their separate togetherness, but she seemed unfazed and talked easily to him. She was pretty but not problematically so—he could tell she'd been an awkward teen too. Lindsay came and sat on Becca's lap, and the two girls talked privately for a minute, their cheeks almost touching. When they went off to the toilets together, he figured that was that. But Becca came back to join him. What did you think? he managed to ask. Seems like the real fear is melody, she said. He wanted to kiss her immediately. He didn't, but soon forgot about his year-long crush on Lindsay.

Becca was his first proper girlfriend. The only ex she'd ever mentioned was Christian, her first. But surely there had been others. In the photographs all over one wall of her room—nights out in fancy dress with girlfriends from home, portraits of her family and late rabbit Snuffles—Christian had featured more prominently than Tom would have liked. A gang of mates, he'd told himself. Mates having a laugh.

By noon, the sun was high and merciless. People moved from one pool of shade to the next, fanning themselves with folded maps. They came to a café with tables outside, all full. A waiter gestured at Becca, inviting her in, smiling wolfishly. 'Five minutes for you, pretty lady. Five minutes you have best table, very best.'

She turned to Tom, her shoulders slumping. 'Can we?'

The pleading note, the sheen of sweat—he fought to deflect the stab of fondness. But, even now, her simplest gestures could overwhelm him. One morning, near the beginning, weak wintry sunlight leaking through the curtains, she had hummed 'Three Blind Mice' while pulling on her tights, and the whole scene had rendered him speechless. Back then, her taste and smell had seemed unsurpassable—he could bury his face in her armpit for days. But, as the months went by, he'd sensed her growing into herself in a way he couldn't match. She began to think and speak more grandly, projecting futures in which his role seemed far from pivotal. Out with friends, he would hear her saying she might head to Melbourne for a year, or apply for a law conversion—ideas she never shared with him.

He'd made tentative suggestions. Travel, work abroad, move to London? She changed the subject, responded vaguely—the long perspective seemed unwelcome. In the end, with graduation looming, the only decision they reached was to retreat to their respective family homes and save for three late-summer weeks in Greece. 'Ruins for me, beaches for you.'

Back on Guernsey, he'd found a temporary government job, pinpointing and photographing the island's fifty-two blue post-boxes for a new digital map. His accomplice was Barnaby, a flatulent, ginger-haired teenager who'd never been further than Alderney and who growled whenever they drove past a girl. At home, his dad and brother were close to killing each other. Tom called Becca every other day, rambling, desperate to prove himself essential. 'Stop ringing her,' his brother said. She was applying for things, she told him—jobs, internships. Can you be more specific? Maybe, she said, if I get one.

From the shaded table outside the café, he could see the Acropolis above the rooftops, stately and unreal. As he watched it floating in the haze, he heard a deep, cigar-wrecked voice in his mind. It belonged to Mr Sheffrin, his old Classics teacher—a blustery, chubby Welshman with long white hair apparently growing in all directions at once. To Tom, he'd seemed resigned to the impossibility of passing on everything he knew. But there was one thing Sheffrin had been determined to make them understand.

'Imagine, gents, a statue almost twelve metres tall, surrounded by Doric columns, standing before a shallow pool that refracts the light and also keeps the ivory moist. Ivory and gold—chryselephantine. Also glass, copper, silver, jewels. Athena Parthenos. Athena the Virgin. Goddess of wisdom, courage, inspiration, civilization, law, justice, mathematics, arts, crafts. Goddess of war. Imagine, gentlemen, a statue more valuable than the Parthenon itself—built specifically, by the way, to house her. More splendid and astonishing than anything the Athenians or anyone else had ever seen. Nike in one hand, shield in the other, with the battles of Theseus, the Amazons and the Giants all carved into it. And on her sandals, perfectly rendered, the mythical show-down between the centaurs and Lapiths.'

Sheffrin had shown slides of artist's impressions, replicas. The original had been swallowed by history, he said, its loss one of the great tragedies of Western culture. Tom, fourteen, had been enthralled that day. How could something so massive, so spectacular, vanish? The other boys, though, were as indifferent as ever, until Sheffrin mentioned 'as an aside' a condition known as agalmatophilia—sexual attraction to statues. 'Takes one to know one, eh, sir?' someone had said. They'd all loved that, of course.

'Are we going up there today?' Becca said, now.

He shook his head, seeing his reflection in her sunglasses. 'Let's save it for the end.'

She nodded, sipped her coffee, scanned the menu. 'What exactly do I want,' she said, quietly, to herself.

They travelled out into the country. The buses were stifling, with shoddy suspension, and the search for a place to stay became more arduous with each passing night. *Souvlákia* were addictive at first but, by the tenth, unpalatable. At dinner, across white-paper tablecloths held in place by metal clips, they sat gazing blankly at people passing by or out at the placid sea.

His blue aluminium water flask, bought for the trip at some expense, began to smell drain-like. Becca refused to drink from it, buying Evian daily with his money. He watched her gulping the cool, fresh water but couldn't give up on the flask.

Among the ruins at Olympia, she lay out on one of the seating ridges, writing postcards while he wandered alone. Later, they tracked down a post-box on the main street of the modern town adjacent to the site. It was bright yellow, with Hermes' profile painted in blue above the words HELLENIC POST. 'This would blow Barnaby's mind,' he said, taking a photograph.

She dropped her cards in. 'Who's Barnaby?' Before he could answer, she ambled away.

One night, arriving late in Argostóli, they found every hotel and hostel full. Close to midnight, they trudged up and down the lamplit harbour, selecting a bench. On the pavement beside it he curled up, offering a sort of apologetic lullaby as she wrapped herself sullenly in a purple sarong. He woke in the night to find a small white dog sniffing at his flask. It pissed on their bags and scampered away. As the sun rose over the hills, he scraped himself up and joined her on the bench. 'We survived,' he said. Saying it made him doubt, for a moment, what he was doing, what he planned to do.

As promised, he paid for everything. Bus tickets, meals, Internet cafés. He loved the texture, the colours, of the euro banknotes, still in their first year of circulation. It felt at once like toy currency and the most serious money he had ever spent. Hotels, snacks, tanning lotions. Her devotion to the sun was total. On the beach she rotated like the hour hand on a clock, pointing her feet at the source.

One day, at a remote Ithakí bay, he swam a way out

and removed his blue checked shorts, floating naked for a while. This became habitual. Soon he was letting the shorts sink, eventually climbing down open-eyed through the warm, clear water to retrieve them. He maintained a mental list of locations where he'd played his little game, which remained a secret until the day came when he couldn't locate the shorts. After almost twenty minutes of searching, he paddled reluctantly shoreward, lingering in the shallows like a pissing child, surrounded by bathers with swimsuits intact, waving to Becca, who was flat on her back, headphones in. At last she sat up and came down to the water. It took her a moment to grasp the situation. She fetched his towel but made him emerge before he could have it, her laughter ensuring that everyone saw.

In the third week, at Myrtos on the south coast of Crete, they argued about the sunscreen he had purchased—the factor was too high, she said. She walked to the water and swam out. He watched her go, thinking they hadn't yet had sex, wondering if they would, if he wanted to. After a while he followed and found her floating naked, bikini bundled in fist. He took her in his arms. She kissed him ravenously and he was quickly inside her, her legs clamped around him as his own kicked madly, trying to keep them afloat. It was all very fierce at first, but soon they were sinking and spluttering. They disentangled and drifted apart, quiet as they clambered back into their suits, legs still flailing under water.

That evening they made sandwiches and took them to

the beach. The sun went down in a frenzy of colour, and as night settled they sipped their beers and listened to the feeble waves. He told her about the Athena Parthenos, the various theories. Destroyed by fire on the Acropolis. Or removed by the Romans and installed in Constantinople, where it stood for another five hundred years before crusaders finally tore it down. Or intercepted somewhere between the two cities, stripped and sold off by common thieves.

'There's other statues, though, aren't there?' she said. 'That survived, I mean.'

Then, in an instant, every light in the village behind them went out. The beach went black. She gasped and reached for his hand. Somewhere, an ecstatic child began to whoop.

'Power cut,' he whispered.

They gathered their things and made their way slowly through the unlit streets. Everything was still. People huddled over candles, murmuring, the small flames shining on their eyes and teeth. Some sang churchy songs. Tom and Becca sat on a low limestone wall and some kittens soon appeared. A black one climbed eagerly into her lap. She leaned forward to whisper into the cat's pink ear.

'Lindsay? Is that you?'

Lindsay. A week before the flight to Athens, she had called him. They hadn't spoken since leaving Leeds— her number wasn't even in his phone. 'We need to talk,' she'd said. 'I spoke with Becs.' Afterwards he sat on the edge of his bed, staring at his knees. Waves of nausea came at him, the floor was falling away. After that, he'd waited for Becca to call off the trip. But she never said a word. By the time he found her waiting at Gatwick, he understood that she never would.

They stayed on that wall with the kittens for what seemed a long time. Eventually, the lamps all flickered back on. People cheered and applauded as delirious children careened through the streets. The kittens scampered away. When he opened up their room and switched on the lights, something important had ended.

Becca shielded her eyes. 'Too bright.'

With two nights to go, they took a ferry back to Athens, stopping overnight at Náxos. Finally at his overdraft limit, he bought the tickets with the last of his cash.

The ferry was packed. Opposite them sat a Greek couple and their sulky son, eleven or twelve years old. The man, overweight with a thick black moustache, stared at the space between Becca's legs. His wife read a romance novel, blowing her hair from her eyes. When the boat stopped at Santoríni, they stood and walked away, taking their bags, the son twenty paces behind.

Some time passed before Tom noticed the wallet on the man's vacated seat. He surveyed the crowded cabin. Becca gazed out of the window, listening to music. As naturally as he could, he made his way to a toilet stall, wallet in pocket. Cards, pristine banknotes, battered passport. At the photo page he found the grim smile of a constipated drinker—Niklos Yannis Valaoritis. He counted one fifty, six twenties, two fives, a total of one hundred and eighty euros. He brought the notes to his nose and inhaled.

He searched every corner of the ferry. The family's seats remained empty. At the railing he stood looking at the water and the islands swimming past, the sky turning pink. When someone pointed out Náxos, he returned to the toilets, emerging from a stall to wash his hands, avoiding his reflection in the mirror.

At the information desk, he explained. The young attendant—crisp white shirt, hair gelled impeccably—turned to the passport's photo page. Tom made a show of studying the image, speculating that the man and his family disembarked at Santoríni. The attendant counted the money in the wallet—forty-five euros.

'Say what, now?' Becca said, when he told her they were nearly there. She seemed not to have noticed he'd been gone. 'You look funny. I'm starving.'

Two words sang out through tinny ceiling speakers—*Niklos Valaoritis*. Tom's chest tightened as he scanned the cabin. He expected to see a finger pointed his way, a unit of crisp-shirted, gel-haired young men advancing. The message was repeated. Lurching to his feet, he grabbed his pack.

'Did they say it's time?' Becca said, stretching languidly.

'Didn't I tell you we were nearly there?'

She recoiled. 'Okay, okay. Jesus.'

From the deck, he saw the harbour lights glowing up ahead. The sky was darkening. He marched to the top of the gated staircase, keeping his face obscured. The ferry slowed, the dock seeming to come no closer as the minutes dragged by. In his pocket he gripped the folded notes. He almost tossed them overboard but, apart from the risk of their blowing back, there was the plan and his need to see it through, no matter the outcome, no matter the cost.

Finally, the gate lifted. He was first down on to the quay, his pack on one shoulder, hers on the other, striding away from the gathered hawkers calling and waving to him. Not until he reached the heart of the town did he slow enough to let her catch up.

At the taverna, he asked for a bottle of white wine and told Becca to order whatever she liked, regardless of price. Second-to-last-night treat, he said. They shared a spread of *mezédhes*, then grilled snapper for him, *moussaka* for her—the best food they'd eaten all trip. The bottle was drained and replaced by another. They talked more freely than on any other night, about Greece, about Leeds, how the last three years had vanished.

She sighed and leaned back in her chair. 'What are we going to do, Thomas?'

She hadn't called him that in months. He refilled their glasses. 'Remember that band the night we met?'

She frowned, one finger held up. 'Don't tell me.' When he did, she reached across to squeeze his hand, knocking over an empty glass.

'It's from Virgil,' he said. 'Aeneas says, *I fear the Greeks, even bearing gifts*. You know the story of the Trojan horse?'

She raised an eyebrow. 'Give me some credit.' Taking

her hand back, she righted the fallen glass. 'Remember that guy, though? The singer? God knows what Lindsay was up to there. Apparently he was really weird in bed. Bad weird, I mean.'

He drank more wine. Tables around them had filled up with diners, locals mostly, a few tourists. Ivy coiled around the beams and in the corner a fountain trickled.

'This was so sweet of you,' she said, pushing her clean plate away. 'The whole trip has been so . . .' She swallowed, looked away. 'You're always so sweet.'

He saw he had to do it then or not at all.

'I have to tell you something,' he said. 'About Lindsay, actually. Something happened.' His voice had become that other man's again. 'Right before we left Leeds.'

She swayed back. 'Something like what?'

'You'd gone. There was hardly anyone left. A few of us went out and it all got a bit—you know.'

He watched as it sank in. Her head moved slowly from side to side. She screwed her eyes shut, wrinkled her nose. 'Did you have sex with her? Is that what you're saying?'

'I'm sorry. I just thought –'

'But she left the day after me!'

His hands were clasped under the table. 'Right. So that night.'

'Straight after I left?' She was almost shouting now. 'Straight the fucking minute I left?' People were turning to look. She covered her face with her hands. 'I can't believe her. She's always saying how you liked her first like it's so fucking funny.'

He checked himself for satisfaction and found none. Finally, she lowered her hands. 'Why are you telling me this?'

'I didn't want to lie.'

The waitress cleared their plates, patting Becca gently on the shoulder. He drank his wine and waited.

'I can't do this,' she said, her voice high-pitched and shaky. She straightened up, lifted her chin. 'I did it too. I slept with someone else.'

Finally. He felt a kick in his chest—hearing it from her was, it turned out, harder than hearing it the first time. 'Who? When?'

'Christian.'

'How many times?'

His lack of surprise seemed to stop her for a moment. 'Only once.'

'Once?'

She looked down at her hands. 'A few times.'

'Do you want to be with him?'

She shrugged. 'Do you want to be with Lindsay?'

'That was –'

'My best friend.'

He fought to steady his voice. 'It's not the same as screwing your ex all summer long.'

Plates of pastries arrived. The waitress glanced between the two of them as if less sure now where her sympathies lay. She took the second empty bottle, not offering another. They sat considering the honey-glazed treats.

'I can't eat any more,' he said at last.

She dabbed at her reddened eyes with a napkin,

collecting mascara smears. 'Oh, Thomas,' she said. 'What are we going to do?'

When he was fifteen, after the appendectomy, he had stayed in the hospital for almost a week. He'd been back at school, though, when the boys returned from Greece. They were all sunburned and brimming with stories, most of which featured 'the German girls'—a party of sixteen-year-olds they'd run into wherever they went. There had been midnight liaisons, illicit beers, lost virginities and other milestones. Sheffrin had been legendary, they said. The trippers acquired immediate stature, swaggering down the corridors like conquering heroes. Tom could only watch and listen, lingering at the circle's edge as tales were recounted, glories relived. He'd wanted to ask, what was it like? But he'd known they would only laugh. It was just some old temple, after all.

At dawn, he and Becca dragged themselves back to the harbour. He told her he had run out of money, and she stopped without a word at an ATM. Weeks later, when it all seemed distant, she would send him a cheque for her half of the trip. Stuck to it would be a yellow Post-it note—*Payback time.* In the bottom right corner, a tiny *x*.

Her silence lasted well into the crossing. 'It's funny,' she said eventually, looking out on the glassy water from their shaded deck seats. 'I told Lindsay about Christian, and she really tore into me. She made me feel terrible. And the whole time –'

At 11 a.m., they docked at Pireás. Back in the Pláka,

they found a cheap hotel. As she paid, she asked for separate beds, but their light-filled top-floor room had only one. They lay apart, turned away, midday city noise straying in through the open windows. When he was certain she had fallen asleep, he slipped out on to the balcony. The skyline of the old town lay out around him, flat roofs and cables, labyrinthine alleys. Above it all towered the Acropolis, treasures obscured by its steep limestone flanks, sky beyond cloudless and decadently blue.

In the bathroom, he splashed his face with cold water, tidied his hair, brushed his teeth. He found her purse and took what he needed. He stood for a moment watching her sleep—her mouth ajar, right knee bent, still in last night's pale green dress. He wanted so badly to kneel beside the bed, rest his face close to hers on the pillow, breathe her in one last time. But if she woke it would all be ruined.

He closed the door silently behind him.

On crowded cobbled streets, blue flask in hand, he joined the westward flow along the northern edge of the rock. He imagined Becca, back at home, next week or maybe sooner, confronting Lindsay, realizing he'd lied. He imagined Odysseus, Diomedes and the others, warriors in the wreckage, victors in the shadow of their hollow horse.

The sun beat down as he climbed towards the Beulé Gate, people around him making their way slowly in the heat. Sweat stung his eyes as he bowed his head. He could feel it taking shape ahead of him—weathered marble, catalogued rubble—and tried to lengthen his stride. He could hear it again, Sheffrin's voice, describing the hole in the Parthenon floor, the vacant spot where Athena once stood. He tried to feel the weight of arriving at last, to think of all the things he was about to see and not just the thing missing, not just the thing lost.

6. Preparation for Trial

Establish remorse from outset. Express bewilderment at sequence of events so unlikely, so absurd and catastrophic. Assure all present of blemish-free record, respect for civic infrastructure, fondness for quiet life and simple pleasures (milkless Earl Grey, sensation of shower on once-dislocated shoulder, smell of wet denim, etc.). Adopt strong posture, upright but unhaughty, chin raised to illustrate mettle. Remain composed.

Nod solemnly when alleged acts detailed. Promise to provide context in form of days preceding—disorientating effect, toll inflicted on sense of self/place in grand scheme/professional trajectory. Blame said effect for alleged recklessness, surrendering to moment, abandonment of principles (loyalty, punctuality, even keel, modesty, graft, appropriate attire, camaraderie). Downplay partiality for music, arts. Highlight childhood aptitude in mathematics, science. Maintain eye contact to correct extent. Avoid long monologues.

Declare intention to act as own legal counsel. Suggest deep knowledge of judicial protocol less important than conveying near-infinite complexity of modern life, pressures of which intolerable. Use as evidence pictures, chanced upon recently, of Earth from space, totally dark but for luminous streaks— flight paths, arcing and meshing across planetary surface, brightest over teeming cities such as ours, sparsest over distant wildernesses beckoning like empty rooms at party hosted by enemy. How to contend? How remain steady before images so stunning, quotidian routine rendered (meaning-wise) scant? How defecate, shower, shave face, commute, toil, defer to superiors, remain polite at sandwich outlet when handsome, better-dressed, wealthier man barges past holding forth into hands-free set, causing spillage of expensive scalding-hot beverage on to newly purchased, freshly ironed shirt?

Resist digression.

Expect prosecution to roll out photograph. Contemplate image, wince, tilt head. Express respect for Bill Pointer and work—recall *The Singing Dunes* tattered copy on Uncle Steve coffee table, youthful hours lost in pages, disbelief such places/people real, magnificence of world revealed. Voice regret current incarceration prevents visit to Pointer retrospective at RGS. State desire to encounter Pointer, shake hand, thank sincerely. With rueful smile, relate compulsive maternal scrapbooking of every traceable picture appearance across international print media—three scrapbooks required, fourth purchased as precaution. Remark on poignant comparison with *Owen's Achievements Book*, maintained by said mother throughout boyhood, pages stuffed with house-point cards, Chess Club certificates, snaps of smiling face atop podiums, on stages with trumpet to mouth, eyes closed. Contrast pride in said achievements with shame of alleged participation in riot, particularly striking of officer in face as captured by Pointer lens.

Shake head. Shuffle papers humbly. Gaze at punch-throwing hand as if at disobedient dog.

*

Begin at beginning re: date with Melissa in week preceding alleged acts. Delineate long-term fondness, years of admiration from across office floor, instances of hopes raised and dashed, cordial gestures (waves, smiles) mistaken for romantic overture. Lay bare '09 Valentine events when, thanks to hopeless courier, dozen immaculate blood-red roses (intended for Melissa) made day if not year of Sharon McGrath, sour colleague without life partner, consumer of canned tuna at desk. Confess transferring of bouquet to intended destination while Sharon in bathroom, Melissa in kitchen making Yorkshire with milk, two sugars. Horror of witnessing, upon return of both, Melissa accused of theft. Exchange of vitriol between women terrible. Later discovery of doomed roses stuffed into kitchen bin, tiny card with tasteful, anonymous message torn into thirds.

Christmas party '10 hardly better. Admit to excessive punch consumption, misguided attempt to engage Melissa on dancefloor, failure witnessed by lion share of colleagues. Final blow—glimpsing, through cab window at party end, Melissa lovingly in Jonathan Appleton arms, company director, family man. Memory unpleasant.

Move swiftly to euphoria, tinged with doubt, of email arrival in July '11, four months after Melissa departure from firm, three since Appleton tragic death during seventh marathon mile. (Conceal at all costs feelings of triumph re: Appleton demise.) Honour private nature of Melissa message. Merely give gist, i.e., date? Ask all present imagine—person of dreams, out of blue, proposes rendezvous. Deploy images of choral angels, golden tickets, divine handshakes, etc., while acknowledging dubiousness. Life to date bereft of such fortune—questions inevitable.

Date arranged for Thursday evening nonetheless.

Describe nervousness in days prior—workplace errors, paltry sleep, near-miss at pedestrian crossing. Outfit selection challenging, patience of several shop assistants tested.

Recall early arrival, unsuccessful attempt to drink Martini without spillage, last-minute switch to less showy beverage. Melissa appearance glorious, beauty incomparable, first embrace all ever imagined. Immediate sidelining of doubt, renewed audibility of angelic choir. Underscore ease of conversational flow, sense of shooting breeze with old best friend plus added sexual charge. (Gloss over sexual charge.) Service fine, food exquisite, lighting and ambience spot on.

Pause. Clasp hands, swallow thickly, dab eyes with handkerchief. Allow all present to contemplate navy-blue M&S suit, unostentatious paisley tie—attire of violent potential reoffender?

Admit failure to notice during giddy first hour Melissa Riesling glass untouched while own glass drained and refilled twice. Disclose result of querying abstinence—tears, apologetic sobs. Feeling of tenderness and concern plus fear. Cut to chase—Melissa with child. First thought—bastard Appleton. (Refrain from speaking ill of dead.) Father in fact French dentist met on holiday, no apparent contact since. Ask all present imagine difficulty of hearing while emphasizing maintenance of even keel. Tenderness for Melissa only heightened, also desire to assist and protect. Confess to visions of domestic bliss—Melissa/child/self hand in hand, skipping through autumnal Regent's Park, kicking up orange and purple leaves, or self returning from hard day toil to embraces from and chats with Melissa/child. Powerlessness before such visions.

Date remainder wonderful. Second Riesling bottle consumed, formation of unbreakable bond apparent. Bill paid by self, generous tip left, Melissa escorted to summery street. Stroll through St Christopher's Place unforgettable—cobbles, al fresco diners, laughter and glasses clinking—streetlight glow on Melissa face sublime.

Repeat verbatim declaration made at Bond Street Station steps. Allow voice to crack, as on night in question. Ensure all present grasp feeling-depth, intention-sincerity. Demand all imagine despondency when declaration met with further tears, shakes of head. Respect Melissa privacy. Merely give gist, i.e., no chance, had hoped to feel something but no, great guy but no, huge mistake, etc. Evoke Melissa descent into station while self in street, buffeted by crowds, faith in universe smashed.

Pause. Allow moment to resonate. Lift chin, state with steady voice—only beginning.

Underscore scarcity of experiences more desolate than Tube ride home. Sombre Roman Road station–flat walk worsened by approach of anxious young woman in minuscule skirt and vest—underweight, facially haggard. Depict deathliness in girl eyes, crookedness of grin. Sexual act offered to self in exchange for contribution to urgent narcotic acquisition. Reassure—proposition declined, attempt made to walk on, head down, without fuss. Confirm girl persistence, provocative phrases hissed into ear, manual interference below belt buckle, quoted price lowered, available acts diversified. Paces widened, confrontation avoided, reluctance to raise hands in aggression—ask be borne in mind.

Building front door finally reached, vanishing of girl down shadowy alley behind Mr Sahid corner shop. Own up to collapse on hallway floor, brief sobbing episode amid strewn junk mail. Detection of neighbourly ears pressed to doors—no well-being enquiry forthcoming. Recount trudging upstairs, squeezing past bicycles, aggressive music emanating from adjacent flat. Residence entered, pockets emptied.

Pause. Shake head wryly (memory unpleasant). Confirm—wallet stolen by street girl.

Skip ahead to following day, mentioning in passing paltry sleep. Sketch unusual office atmosphere—palpable tension, nervous jocularity, whisperings re: revenue. Recall seeing junior colleague shuffle into meeting room, emerge grey of face, gather things and depart. Surmise own fate suddenly apparent. Suspicion soon confirmed—called in, informed with regret must be let go, thanked for service, blame laid squarely at feet of credit crunch/recession. Liken slow return to desk to stroll through submerged aquarium tunnel, murderous sharks raking teeth against glass. Worst culprit—Sharon McGrath.

Ensuing hours a blur—dumping of desk box, roaming of streets, consumption of real ales in unidentified establishments, extended nap on London Fields bench, throwing of jagged pebbles at graceful, blameless ducks. Detection of malevolence at work in city, world, galaxy. Failure to discern positive forces operating in any life aspect. Yearning for Melissa, interrogation of point/meaning, eventual return to dwelling.

Pause. Sip from water if available. Inhale deeply, check posture, meet eyes. Impart via demeanour—crux imminent.

Describe watching Tottenham riots on live news channel deep into night. Remark none more surprised than self to note nascent participatory desire. Concede desire related less to ostensible cause than to sense of boiling point almost reached. Draw attention to admirable decision to retire rather than travel to scene.

Acknowledge own scepticism re: dream interpretation while insisting dream dreamed on night in question deserving of consideration. Spare details—give gist, i.e., extravagant sexual congress with Melissa, wondrous sensation of togetherness/love. Request imagine devastation of waking late Sunday morning to realize all mere fiction. Request further imagine strangeness of discovering riot scene now directly outside window.

Concede hesitation re: joining fracas minimal. Put in simple terms—one minute in bed, next pyjama-clad in street throwing bottles.

Liken simultaneous terror and elation to ecstatic childhood trances—staring cross-eyed at patterned wallpaper in parental bedroom (parents not home) repeating mantra along lines of *this really happening* until blissfully overwhelmed by ferocious cascading unshakeable sense of self presence in space/time. Alternative, weaker metaphor—if condemned to burn alive, better be at hottest part of fire.

Make clean breast—alleged participation in riot perhaps most thrilling moment of year if not life. But accompanying remorse, guilt, shame?

Pause. Mop brow. Request Pointer photograph again be rolled out. Regard image in silence for minimum one minute. Describe as if all present blind—pyjama-clad self, face contorted, striking officer with fist while second officer moves to restrain. Suggest self unrecognizable but indeed self. In background, flame-engulfed corner shop where low-fat milk, *Sunday Times*, whole-wheat bread regularly purchased. Voice regret re: Mr Sahid—nicest man ever met, always forthcoming with kind greeting, working all hours at health expense, forced to rebuild livelihood from scratch. Declare Mr Sahid and ilk undeserving of such.

Hang head, press palms together. Apologize from heart-bottom. Request leniency. Suggest all seek out (prior to judgement) aforementioned images of flight paths from space, ponder, note change in mood/perspective. Speculate images confirm point/meaning unknowable—all lives arcing, luminous, meshed.

Turn to gallery. See mother, scrapbooks in canvas bag. See Mr Sahid smiling, giving thumbs-up. Beside him, Melissa, dozing infant in arms. Bellow devotion, tears streaming, arms aloft. Declare willingness to kill if required. Perceive approving glimmer on Melissa face as guards surge forward to shackle wrists, tackle to ground, blows raining down on skull and torso as dragged kicking from courtroom to rapturous applause. Hear sweet Melissa voice amid cacophony, promising to wait, remain loyal, endure, she will wait, oh my love, she will wait, she will wait.

7. The Hosepipe Ban

The first conversation with Flora took place over the garden fence. Later it would strike him as their only conversation, and later still he would come to believe that they had never really talked at all—at least, not properly, one adult to another. Which, of course, technically, she wasn't at the time. But it might as well have been the other way around.

Saturday, early September. Roger sweated in shorts in the garden, reading *The Times*, using it to shield his face from the sun. He'd already discarded the day's *Guernsey Press*, which lay beside his shaky deckchair. The boys were inside on the computer, Lucy busy unpacking another box. He had ten more minutes, he guessed, before she came out needing help. The sky was a flawless molten blue, no cloud in sight that might end the drought. Butterflies and bees called on stricken flowers at the edge of the khaki lawn.

That summer of '89 had been the driest he'd known. The reservoir was almost empty—he'd driven by and witnessed the exposed banks and protruding reeds, frightened to see it so low. The next day, he'd gone back with Lucy and the boys to make sure they understood. They'd all been sharing bathwater for weeks, flushing no more than four times a day, but it didn't feel like enough.

The *Marchioness* dead still littered the national headlines, a week since it went down, and Roger tried to think about those rich kids in the Thames, about drowning in a summer so parched.

Instead he thought again about yesterday's meeting. When called upon to speak, he had made a slip—'Not a ginormous problem,' he'd said—that caused him to twitch and sip from an empty water glass. It was one thing to pick this stuff up from the boys, another to repeat it in a stifling room full of colleagues senior and otherwise. And, of course, it would be *ginormous*. 'Not a real word!' he'd pointed out time and again, in the same voice he used to critique their enunciation. 'A *gnu* is an animal, you animals. Now tell me again what you're *going to* do.'

Thankfully, no one in the States of Guernsey accounting department seemed to care. Nobody, that is, but old Doug Le Huray, flabby and red-faced bowls enthusiast, who later that day shared with Roger his plan to barbecue a fish for tea. The fish in question, Doug pointedly said, was a 'ginormous' skate, hooked off the south coast by his son-in-law.

Good one, Doug. Watch out for bones—a man could choke. In his deckchair, Roger tried not to think about work, to focus instead on the interesting paper and the sun warming his bare, unmuscular chest. Sounds of laughter and rushing water began drifting over the fence. Was that a hosepipe? Surely not. He'd met the neighbours, or the parents at least—they'd knocked to say welcome the day of the move. Nice people, mid-forties.

Though their house was ostensibly identical to this one, they'd done it up at great expense—new roof tiles, new guttering, huge new conservatory out the back—and, in the process, made this one look decidedly scruffy. Lucy hadn't taken to them, but that was hardly unusual. Roger had spotted the daughter a few times, leaving the house or coming home in her Ladies' College uniform. The deep-green blazer and tartan skirt were no less intimidating now, at thirty-eight, than they had been two decades earlier. To a Grammar boy, that uniform sent a clear message—the girl was either richer or cleverer than you, and very possibly both.

Lucy emerged through the back door, hand up to shade her eyes. 'Can I borrow you?' she called. 'Heavy box.'

Still unpacking, five weeks since the move. He had done his part, he felt, shifting the furniture, installing the stereo, shelving his records, setting up the TV and Spectrum ZX to keep the boys amused. His first and most important task, though, had been identifying the small, unmarked box full of Babygros, burp cloths and dummies that had belonged to their daughter, Imogen. Their first, she'd lived for only four months. Double pneumonia, which at the time a doctor described to them as a kind of drowning from within. Roger had taken that little box up to the big bedroom and stashed it under the eaves, right at the back in a dark corner where the roof met the floor, safe, locatable if necessary, impossible to chance upon.

He stood up and listened more intently, moving towards the fence. Damn thing needed creosoting—add it to the list. The phone rang and he saw Lucy head back inside. Close to the fence was the stump of an elm seen off by the Dutch disease. He stepped up on to it and peered over.

He saw a paddling pool, a foot or so deep, stiff plastic sides checked blue and white. In the pool crouched a girl with a blonde perm. She hugged her knees, all arms and legs, black swimsuit barely visible. The hose was held by another girl, tall and slender, in sunglasses and a swimsuit with pink-and-white stripes. This was the daughter, the one he had seen. The absence of uniform did nothing to lessen the waves of danger emanating out of her. Intensified them, in fact. She tossed her dark hair from her face and flicked the hose so that the torrent splashed on to her friend.

'Don't!' shrieked the girl with the perm. 'It's cold!'

Roger stood rigid at the fence. Speak up or duck down? Sudden movement might draw attention. Speaking certainly would. The longer he went unnoticed, the seedier he became. Finally the girl with the perm looked up. 'Shit!' she said, bringing one hand to her chest. The tall girl turned her head calmly, hose still aimed at pool, eyeing him—he could feel it—through her glasses. Passing the hose from one hand to the other, she turned, swimsuit straps hanging down off her shoulders. 'All right there, mister neighbour?' she said.

'Sorry, I—didn't mean to scare you—I heard the hose going and thought maybe you didn't know about the ban? The hosepipe ban, I mean.'

The girl with the perm, still crouching, stifled a laugh.

The tall girl looked down at the hose in her hand, then back up at Roger. 'The hosepipe ban,' she said, as if tasting the phrase. 'What's your name, then?'

He chuckled strangely and shrugged, suddenly aware of his own scrawny shoulders, pale, so much hairier these last few years. The girl with the perm laughed again. 'It's Roger.'

'Roger that. I'm Flora. That's Fauna.'

He raised his hand lamely.

'Obviously,' Flora went on, 'that's not her *actual* name.' Fauna stepped out of the brimming pool and walked across the lawn to the tap. The hosepipe went limp in Flora's hand, and she dropped it to the grass. 'How is it, Faun?'

'Rather chilly,' Fauna said, putting on a mannered voice. A little joke of theirs? 'But most pleasant.' Flora turned back to Roger. Her glasses caught the light and flashed. 'Sorry, darling, you were saying?'

Behind him he heard crunching footsteps. Turning, he saw Lucy, head tilted and hugging herself, gazing off, standing between house and lawn on the gravel he'd promised to replace with crazy paving.

'Roger?' Flora's hands were on her hips. 'You were saying?'

He waved again. 'Nothing major.' *Nothing major?*

She stepped into the pool. In her assured, dismissive smile, he glimpsed her whole life—money, love, happiness, handsome children, nights in Europe's finest hotels. Those poor rich kids on that ferry, dancing one minute, sinking the next. He turned and went to his wife.

'Luce? Who was that?'

Arms still crossed, Lucy looked at him as if from a long way away. 'That was Mum.' Her wet eyes shone, her voice small. 'Apparently Dad's . . .' She shook her head. 'Apparently he's . . .'

He put his arms around her. Her red hair smelled like it needed a wash. Only once Ned's first birthday had safely come and gone had she begun to resemble the girl Roger remembered, the girl he'd brought back to his island after university—the girl who spoke her mind, who drank Guinness like a bloke and laughed from somewhere south of her lungs. Only once the boys were both at school and she had found a job at Candie Museum did he allow himself to believe that they might still carve out a happy life. This new, bigger house on Jerbourg Road seemed to offer further proof. In St Martin's, no less, the sought-after parish, less than a mile from the cliffs. Double-glazing already installed. But now she was mumbling something into his chest that he couldn't quite make out. He could still hear the splashing, the stifled laughter, carrying over the fence.

It was a stroke. A bad one. She left the next day to be at his bedside, flying to Gatwick and then taking the train up to Nottingham, ready to stay as long as required in the house where she'd grown up.

Roger dropped the boys with his mother in the mornings, retrieving them on his way home from the office. She stuffed them so full of after-school cake that he could usually get away with serving cheese on toast or Micro Chips for tea. Doug Le Huray was off all week with food poisoning, leaving Roger with a pile of extra work. He took some comfort in imagining that his boss's troubled guts could be blamed on undercooked skate.

Always a risk with the barbecue, Doug.

On Thursday evening, the woman next door came around to say she and her husband were off to Saint-Malo for the weekend. Would Roger mind keeping an eye on things while they were gone? If there's a party, she said, feel free to call the police. He laughed, then realized it wasn't a joke. He told her his wife was away too—he had his hands full. But no, of course, that was absolutely fine.

On Saturday, the boys rose early and eager. Breakfast was dominated by anticipation of that afternoon's air display, plus approval of the favourable weather—last year, the display had been cancelled due to fog. Would there be Spitfires? If a pilot ejects, does his plane keep flying or smash into innocent bystanders and explode? The exact number of Red Arrows was disputed at length until Roger was called on to settle it.

'Nine? Nine when they're in formation, at least. No doubt they've got a couple of spares in the hangar.'

'Told you,' said Ned.

'I'm basically nine,' said Tom, dark-haired, serious.

'*Almost* or *nearly*,' Roger said, smearing shredless marmalade on to their toast.

'You only just turned eight!' said Ned.

Talk turned to possible vantage points. Tom announced

that he wanted to feel the jets flying right past his face. Don't be ridonkulous, his brother said. Should they go soon to bag a good spot? Roger insisted there was plenty of time and, besides, he had business to attend to on the roof. As they carried their dishes across to the sink, pushing each other playfully, he realized as if for the first time that these boys belonged unchangeably to him. Easy to forget when their mother was around—the three of them talking and giggling without him, office stuff leaving him distracted and ratty—but in these few days fending for themselves it had struck him anew with not-unpleasant force.

He got them settled in the living room, cross-legged before the Spectrum ZX. Roger regarded the cardboard boxes still piled in the fireplace left vacant when the previous owners (cheeky sods) pinched the vintage woodburning stove for their new farmhouse out west. Maybe later he'd have time to unpack one or two.

'If anyone needs me, I'll be up on the roof.'

They were already entranced, breathing uneven, mouths hanging open, black plastic joysticks creaking in their fists. This football game had been the obsession ever since he took them to the Muratti—the annual match against Jersey—on Liberation Day. Guernsey had lost, as usual, 4–0. He'd hoped to inspire zeal for the actual sport, not just a computerized simulation. But at least they'd stopped chanting 'Red and white! You are shite!' at all hours of the day—a refrain picked up in the stands, much to their mother's consternation. He'd managed to get them out of there before things really got ugly, though they were apparently too devastated by the defeat to notice the aggro escalating all around them.

In the shed, he surveyed his meagre collection of tools and materials. Progress so far had been minimal. There were bathroom tiles coming loose, a banister near collapse, a light switch or two in need of rewiring. Lucy's father, who'd built his own family home from scratch, had often humiliated his son-in-law with a casual reference to the younger man's hopelessness with DIY. Now Roger vowed to prove himself, to get this place in shape for his wife's return. First, a straightforward, high-impact task—painting the chimney stack.

From the rooftop, the morning looked benevolent, sprawled out beneath him. Attired in old shorts and a Swimarathon T-shirt damp at the pits, he trod with care across the tiles, fair hair darkened by sweat. In his left hand he carried a bucket of paint, lid prised open but not yet removed, and in his right a ragged paintbrush with fraying bristles. His arms were outstretched for balance, not because he expected to fall but to heighten the feeling of precariousness.

Up close, the old paint looked even worse. No clay chimney pot protruded from the stack, the shaft merely ending or beginning as a hole. As he contemplated his task, a ferocious, whooshing roar erupted overhead. He ducked instinctively, still clutching the brush, cowering with his hands at his head, twisting to watch the howling red dart pierce the sky and vanish. Straightening up, fringe now embellished with paint, he called down the chimney to the boys. 'They're warming up if you want to see?'

He began to feel watched. In the garden next door, he noticed, Flora lay on a white plastic lounger, long hair pulled back off her face. Her arms rested at her sides, palms down. Black sponge headphones covered her ears, wired to a Walkman lying on the grass. She had the thing turned up so loud that he could make out the tinny, insistent beat of whatever she was listening to. One tanned and slender leg was raised at the knee, straps down off her shoulders again. Her face seemed angled towards him, but like last time her sunglasses made it hard to tell. She was watching him, he felt certain—why else the surge of blood to his cheeks?

He waved. She didn't move. Asleep? Probably asleep. Otherwise she would've waved. Wouldn't she?

'Daaa-ddy, Daaa-ddy!' The boys' voices, sing-song, emerged from the chimney. 'We can see-ee you!'

He peered down into the darkness but couldn't make them out. 'Get away from there,' he called down, though he couldn't have said why. He took the lid from the bucket and dipped his brush into the viscous white paint. He slopped it on imprecisely. Spots drizzled the tiles at his feet—who would ever know? When rogue blobs plummeted, he caught them with a flourish. 'Daaa-ddy, Daaa-ddy!' The sky filled with a heavy, trembling growl. Looking up, he saw what seemed to be a Lancaster bomber. He shielded his eyes and watched the great old thing sail over, its shadow engulfing the house for a moment. In its wake the morning seemed to gather back into itself, like the water at Fermain growing calm again after the waves sent in by a passing ferry.

The bomber flew on and Roger lowered his hand, but before he could even reload his brush there came another apocalyptic howl—another Red Arrow. It had passed before he could even react, but still he recoiled as if under attack, his movements involuntary. The sound was astonishing, even louder than the first. It subsided quickly, but he stayed crouching, braced for another assault.

'All right up there, mister neighbour?' she shouted, louder than needed, headphones still in place.

He straightened quickly, twisting his body, flinging up an arm to wave down to her. He felt the bucket go as he hit it, not toppling and tipping its contents out but dropping straight down the sooty shaft, still upright, still full of paint. But he was waving before he truly realized. And it wasn't until the screams blasted up through the chimney that he understood what had happened.

He dropped the brush, flailed across the pantiles and jumped.

In the living room, Ned was on his feet and yelling, paint strewn across his torso and arms, gripping his brother and pulling him up. Tom was silent, his chest, neck and face all smothered, his hands, themselves completely white, clawing at his nose and mouth. Through the paint, Roger could see the curve of eyelids, slicked shut. Ned was shrieking 'Tommy! Daddy!' over and over. Without a legible thought in his head, Roger picked them up, one under each arm, and surged across the hallway, through the kitchen and out the back door. Flinging them on to the dead grass, he tore open the shed door, and from right in the back, where he had coiled and stashed it on the basis that he couldn't use it even if he wanted to, he retrieved the blue hosepipe, unspooling it as he marched to the outside tap. The connector was suddenly hell to attach. Ned screaming terribly. Roger cursed his useless, fumbling hands until finally the threads lined up and he could screw the thing on and twist the tap, watching the pipe swell and kick as the water went coursing through.

By the time the nurse called his name, rushing them in had begun to feel excessive. But he needed reassuring— forgiving, really. The nurse listened closely with her eyebrows raised and smiled at Tom, prodding him once in the arm. 'S'pose your dad forgot there's a hosepipe ban, eh?'

The hospital had added a new wing for children since Imogen died. Still, he couldn't help thinking of that time, the harrowing nights, Lucy lashing out, eyes bloodshot and half deranged. She had blamed the doctors, convinced in her grief that a mainland hospital could have saved her baby, that this backwards island he'd dragged her to was cursed, a hellhole, a non-place. At her worst, her most adamant, he was almost persuaded. But he knew there was nothing anyone could have done, that their daughter just wasn't cut out to live, that death would have found her wherever she'd been.

'Sorry you missed the display,' he said, once they were back at home. Both boys shrugged. What troubled them was the Spectrum's demise—they followed behind in a sombre procession as he carried the paint-caked console and joysticks out to the bin. He looked at their downcast faces. 'Should I say a few words?'

The carpet was ruined, the fumes intolerable. It was all over the granite fireplace too—no idea what to do about that. He took them out to Cobo for fish and chips. Sitting on the seawall, he watched them eating, fanning their mouths, forming Os with their lips. As the sun went down, they skimmed stones, or tried to—Tom grew frustrated, couldn't get the knack. Roger counted Ned's bounces aloud, nine, ten, eleven, twelve. Nothing was said of the incident until the drive home after dark. They were waiting at a red light and the tape was changing sides.

'Dad painted us,' Tom said quietly, as if to himself.

Ned giggled first. His brother joined in and then Roger was laughing too, deep heaving guffaws, tears streaming. The light turned green and the van behind honked. He honked back and that made them laugh even harder. At home, they agreed not to mention anything to their mother until she got home from her trip. They shook on it and he put them to bed—they were sharing the second bedroom until the third was decorated, another job on his list. Ned was grumpy—he wasn't tired yet, why should he go to bed at the same time as an eight-year-old? 'You can stay up tomorrow,' Roger said. 'It's been a bit of a day.' There were still dry flecks of paint in Tom's hair, but Roger was too tired to get him in the bath now. He pulled the door to and stood for a while, forehead resting on the cool wood frame.

Downstairs he poured a glass of cheap red wine and drank it quickly, standing in the kitchen, looking at the phone. When Lucy had called that morning, she'd sounded shattered. Just waiting now, she said. He's hardly breathing. I'll call when he's—you know. I'll let you know.

He refilled his glass and took it into the living room, slumping on the sofa. The house was still. He could hear the refrigerator humming. The cloying paint lay on everything, the air thick with it, so noxious it was almost sweet. He thought about the dropped brush still up on the roof. Had Flora seen him jumping off? Had she heard all the commotion over the racket in her headphones? He pictured the scene from above, from up by the chimney stack. In one garden, a crazed man hosing down his sons, while, in the other, an oblivious, half-naked girl tapped her fingers to whatever beat. His eyelids sagged and the weird thoughts of oncoming sleep began to flow. Sure enough, she was there in the reeling images, uniformed, crooning in French through a loo-roll tube, laughing at some unrepeatable joke, unearthly landscape of gorse and old carousels stretching away behind.

Minutes or was it hours later, he was woken by sounds outside—a car pulling up, door being slammed, tearful expletives and the car roaring off, bassy music thumping. His mouth was dry and vinegary. He heard the clatter of heels as the security light out front came on. Through the window beyond his decrepit reflection he saw her—was it possible?—coming up the driveway, arms across her chest, mascara all smeared, unsteady on her feet. Before he could think, she was knocking on the door.

He stood up but moved no further. His heart kicked alarmingly. He closed his eyes and rubbed them, congealed paint under his fingernails. The knock at the door came again, louder this time.

Hardly breathing, he moved into the hallway, somnambulant, arms out as if going blindly through a cave though all the lights were on. There she was, warped by the decorative glass. He could see the white of her teeth. He fumbled with the latch and opened up, as the phone began to ring.

He was nearly sixty when he saw her, years later, down on the beach at Port Soif.

Lucy was long remarried by then, back up in the Midlands with a chiropractor called Terry. The boys had moved away. He'd resigned a few months earlier, taking the hit for someone else's cock-up. Gallingly simple, really—a fake letter sent to a junior in the department, updating the bank details of a contractor soon to be paid well over a million pounds. Roger never even saw the letter until after the fraud came to light. But a scapegoat was needed and, as a manager closing in on retirement, he was apparently the obvious choice. The *Press* loved it, kept it front page for a week. *Ozanne's Negligence Costs Taxpayers Dearly. Accountant Held Accountable as Ozanne Quits.* So that was that. Thirty-five years of dutiful service, ending in public humiliation, an only-half-decent payoff and more idle time on his hands than was healthy. Thank God old Doug wasn't around to see it.

It was a hot Sunday in August—one of the few good

spells of weather they'd had—and the sand was packed from one end of the bay to the other. Usually he avoided the west coast on days like that, weekends especially, preferring spots like Fermain, where the steep walk down kept the hordes away. But lately his knee had been giving him gyp and he couldn't face the climb back up.

After an hour or two, he'd had enough. He packed up his towel and paper, buttoned his shirt and made his way over to the dozen narrow steps that led up over the rocks to the car park. An endless stream of people was coming down, and with a couple of others he waited at the bottom for someone to do the decent thing. Looking over the water to the stacks marking the southern edge of the bay, he could make out some kids perched up on the highest, steeling themselves to make the jump. He'd made it himself once, a lifetime ago. Now it would probably kill him.

A girl came down the steps, fourteen or so, wearing a wide-brimmed sun hat and a look of abject boredom. Extremely familiar, she was, but before he could try to place her, his eye was caught by the woman behind. Whether or not it was the daughter in front that enabled him to recognize the mother, he couldn't be sure. But it was her, certainly it was her. It was Flora.

She must have been forty now, more or less. Her white shirt and denim shorts were simple but expensive-looking, and she carried herself in the same way, shoulders back, chin up. She looked like she ran a few miles every morning. He couldn't turn away as she came down the steps, graceful, composed, almost floating like the ghost she was. When she reached the sand, she glanced up, and through her big sunglasses he sensed that, for a moment, her eyes met his. Something passed between them, he felt, some acknowledgement of that unreal night long ago when he had dreamed of her and then woken to find her at his door, astonishingly willing, insistent, even. He had never forgotten it, the taste of her mouth, how bewildered and grateful he felt as she pushed him gently back on to the sofa. It hadn't counted, somehow, as a mistake or transgression, and not only because he had hurried her out before anything really happened—before the sleepy voice calling down from upstairs became a boy in his pyjamas, asking if it had been Mummy on the phone. No, it hadn't counted as an act of betrayal, maybe because he'd never had to explain it to anyone but himself.

'Life can be difficult.' He remembered saying that to Ned once, in the little kitchen of the old house, up in the Vale. He must have been barely three then, Ned, his chops all smeared with mash and baked beans. Lucy had taken Tom, still a baby, upstairs for his bath. Roger had been clearing the table when Ned had asked, out of the blue, if his little brother would 'go dead' like Imogen. Roger had assured him that Tom was fine. But Imogen not fine, Ned had said—Imogen go dead, before. Your brother is fine, Roger said, voice catching slightly. Ned didn't ask why Imogen died, but Roger continued as if he had. 'Life can be difficult, Neddy. And it doesn't always make sense. But things line up all right in the end.' At the time, those words had felt like proof of some wisdom, some lofty knowledge he had earned and nurtured, a solid truth to pass down. But it had just been something to say, hadn't it? It didn't mean a thing.

Someone stopped at the top of the steps and waved up the people at the bottom. Roger could hear the wash of breaking waves and the happy shrieks of children swimming. He almost turned to watch her walk away across the sand. But he didn't dare. He didn't dare look in case she wasn't really there.

8. Queen of the Forest

Her flying days were the happiest of my mother's life. She told me that one night when they drove down to Berkeley for dinner. She overdid the Margaritas and eventually bawled, blowing her nose into my napkin. It was February and I was a senior at Cal. My father chewed his rare steak doggedly. She also said she'd been putting money aside for me since I was small, and I could have it when I graduated on the condition that I spent it in London. Whatever happens, she told me, don't get stuck. Why London? I asked, but she didn't say. Just squeezed my arm hard enough to hurt.

It wasn't a million bucks or anything, but it was enough. I flew over the following August, right after the riots, and rented a room in a Lewisham flat with two Polish girls who acted like I wasn't there. For a while I thought maybe they were right. I'd enrolled in a Development Studies MA at South Bank, figuring I'd have my British fun then take my newfound worldliness and wisdom off to some remote country in Africa or Central America, improve the world and maybe in turn be improved. But the fun proved elusive, at first anyway. There was a Spanish guy in the programme that I liked, but I slept with him too soon and that was that. At weekends I loitered in the free museums—the V&A and Natural History were best for burning time. In the Tate Modern gift shop one afternoon, I picked up a flyer for Ghost Walks and read it later sitting on a bench by the river, listening to a busker play 'Wish You Were Here' on a weathered mandolin. While he counted his change, I made the call.

At the Monument I found an agitated guy in a yellow Ghost Walks windbreaker, talking on his phone. I read all the names on the plinth, one dead soldier after another, wondering about the urge to build such things. The windbreaker guy said his name was Tom, that it was meant to be me and a Japanese family and now it was just me. Was that okay? He was tall and skinny with nice, sad eyes, late twenties, maybe thirty. 'Sure,' I said, 'more ghosts for yours truly,' like *yours truly* was something I said all the time. 'What's your position on monuments?'

We set off, everything smothered in the wintry gloom. He told me he used to be obsessed with Ancient Greece, but now London history was more his thing. At first it was awkward to walk like that, side by side with him slowing his long-legged strides. He took me through churchyards full of mossy old headstones, down alleys I would never have chanced alone, where Victorian urchins had met grizzly ends. After an hour we were just talking. Or he was, mostly. He ranted for a while about Facebook, how everyone claimed to be so connected now when in fact they were lonelier than ever. 'If I ever sign up,' he said, 'you have permission to kill me.' Which, now that I think about it, was sort of presumptuous. Then he went on about some playwright he'd known when he was a kid—the guy had recently drunk himself to death. I'd never heard of him, but that didn't seem to matter. I kept glancing across as he talked. His eyebrows, I noticed, never moved, smiling or otherwise. That perfect stillness in the top part of his face was strangely reassuring.

We finished the tour in Green Park, standing over a plague pit, which I let him describe until the thought of all those bodies started to stress me out. Outside the station he commenced a clumsy goodbye. I imagined my lonely journey home, some crappy movie on my laptop in bed, and found myself saying let's go get a drink. He stood there, traffic piling by, this look on his face like the only reason he'd taken that job was in the hope that this moment would eventually come.

'Raise neither eyebrow for yes,' I said.

Last week, when my parents picked me up from SFO, they took me directly to the Golden Peak. My father made it sound like some homey little place, operated by an elderly couple that still held hands, and assured me I'd be more enthused once I saw the buffet. The car, a shaky Civic maybe twelve years old, is not the one they had when I left. But I was still too stupid from the flight to ask.

All cleavage and lip gloss, our waitress greeted my father with a smile I didn't love. They embraced and she kissed him practically on the mouth. My mother, I noticed, was looking elsewhere.

The waitress was named Gloria. She was forty-five or

so, made up like her life depended on it. 'Maggie!' she said, lunging toward me. '*So* great to finally meet you!'

She led us across the vast restaurant, past abandoned tables strewn with plates of half-eaten food. The diners seemed distressed, vexed by an error they couldn't recall making. My father, balder and twenty pounds heavier than when I left, was hailed, hand-shaken, fist-bumped and high-fived by assorted members of staff. We sat by a floor-to-ceiling window with a view up into the Sierras. 'Welcome back to gold country, pardner,' he said, putting on what I guessed was supposed to be an old-timey prospector voice, though he sounded more like a pirate. 'Gold in them thar hills, yessir.'

People wandered from station to station, bearing their heaped plates reverently. A woman in sweatpants and a 49ers T-shirt lost her grip and watched blankly as spring rolls, wings and inch-thick steak slapped wetly on to the tiles. With admirable poise, she laid her plate face down over the steaming pile, adjusted her sweatpants and began again.

I was ready to be in bed. I also had questions. Sometime last year, for reasons that were yet to be explained, my parents sold their house in Carmichael and moved up into the foothills.

Gloria presented a bottle of wine—an '05 Zin, she called it.

'Fabulous,' my father said, to my knowledge for the first time ever.

'Fabu-louse and on the house,' Gloria said. Then she whispered something in his ear that had him leaning back and laughing with his eyes screwed shut. My mother turned away, gazing east through the wall of glass. I went back up to Asian Delights for more.

After dinner, my father led us up the escalators into the huge stale cavern of the gaming floor. The banks of machines seemed endless. Players sat entranced, faces bathed in chaotic light, cigarettes burning down untouched. Each machine emitted its digital babble, amounting to a kind of symphonic white noise that actually wasn't unpleasant. I was signed up, free credit loaded on to my card in honour of my virgin status. My father guided us to his lucky machine, inserted my card and struck buttons adamantly as symbols appeared and vanished. The screen hurt my eyes so I watched him instead. What I saw—eyes wide, mouth open, skin slick—was presumably a kind of rapture. In three minutes, he was up one hundred and twenty-eight dollars.

'Cash out!' my mother cried, a little loudly, I thought.

Later, in the restroom, I watched her in the mirror as we washed our hands. She looked asymmetric, the opposite of airbrushed.

'Dad's like royalty around here, huh?'

She paused in her soaping to meet my reflected gaze. 'Royalty?' That's when I started to realize what it means to be a valued customer at a casino.

In the car, my father talked excitedly. 'It's all computerized these days. High-tech to let first-timers win—to get them hooked, right? But think about it. Sign up with a new fake ID every time and you'd make a killing!'

'Are you hooked, Maggie?' my mother said.

Ten minutes on the highway and we were turning off, winding through forest, past houses set back and obscured. I saw the glow of lit windows and wondered about the lives inside. Honestly, I didn't really know where we were. Not Carmichael. The road narrowed with each bend until we were on a gravel track, at the end of which stood two buildings, separated by unmown grass and an insubstantial wire fence. The clearing was enclosed by shadowy trees. Even in the dark, it was apparent that one of these houses was spectacular, the other a wreck.

'Let me guess,' I said.

Inside, bare bulbs hung on cables. Sections of wall were gaping, loose wires splaying out. The living room had underlay but no carpet and the kitchen had no floor at all save for some planks laid across the foundations. The cabinet door underneath the sink was missing and buckets were catching drips.

Handing me a headlamp, my father led me upstairs into darkness.

'No power up here yet,' he said. 'But dark's good for sleeping in, right?'

I decided not to argue with that. He brought my suitcases up, patted my shoulder collegially, and left the room in what struck me as kind of a hurry.

My bedroom seemed small, though it was hard to tell. My headlamp illuminated familiar things—same comforter on same bed, same stuffed animals tucked in—and with my beam reaching into the darkness I felt like a diver swimming through the sunken wreckage of my childhood. On my dresser sat the little piece of petrified redwood I've had since I was eleven. On the wall hung my old mirror with stickers on the frame and the photo of my mother on Primrose Hill. She's twenty in that picture, five years younger than me now, an American Airlines flight attendant back when the job still had some class. She's never told me who took it, but from the way she's smiling you can tell it was a guy. Somewhere on my hard drive is a photo Tom took of me, posing in the same spot. The thing I like most is the hat she's wearing—something between a beret and a trilby—though the colour of it isn't clear.

She came in later to say goodnight, wearing a head-lamp of her own. When we hugged, my beam lit up the space behind her and hers lit up the space behind me.

By the summer, Tom and I had moved into a one-bed place in Dalston. He had a smooth appendectomy scar on his belly that I loved to run my fingertip over while we lay in bed and asked each other about our lives. Weekends we met his friends in the park and drank Magners in the feeble sun. Or we went to Tate Modern to stare at the Rothkos. Or, once, to the Royal Geographical Society for a show by some old photojournalist he was excited about. This is it, I thought—real London. I worked on changing my accent, deploying little phrases—*to be fair, not bothered, can't be arsed, need a wee* instead of *have to pee*. I could feel the city opening up. Most of the people I met had moved for college or after, but considered themselves locals anyway, talking like they'd roamed through Spitalfields as kids, like they were never going to leave. I got it. I wanted Carmichael to be a distant fragment of my past, something that might come up over dessert at a dinner party in Kensal Green. *You'll never believe where Maggie grew up* . . . I thought of my mother at twenty, a wide-eyed California girl seeing the world. I'd fallen for the city like she did. The only difference was, I *wanted* to be stuck.

When my course wrapped up, most of my classmates went off to work or volunteer in countries with wars or famines in full swing. I wound up waiting tables in a Pizza Express off Baker Street. The Olympics cleared the city out, replacing all the Londoners for three or four weeks with a weird breed of tourist. The American ones sometimes looked at me funny—you're from the States, right? No, I'd say, why do you ask?

Tom took me to Guernsey to meet his father and show me his strange little island, with its tiny chapel covered in plate shards and seashells and its clifftop Nazi bunkers. His father kept calling me Margaret Thatcher—to be fair, I wasn't bothered. We went up to Nottingham a couple of times too, to stay with his mother. The second time, her husband offered to adjust my spine, an offer I stupidly declined. The only one I never met was his brother, Ned, who was always travelling or working abroad—mostly in Africa, as far as I could tell.

The months slunk happily by until the end of my visa began to loom. Two years after graduation was the deal, and those two years were almost up.

That spring, we took the train up to Leeds for a reunion of Tom's old college friends. He'd heard about it at the last minute—the Facebook boycott was still intact. He warned me his ex would be there, and when we walked into the pub and I scanned all the girls, I had to laugh. Let me guess, I said. She was taller, hair a bit shorter, but I recognized the shape of my mouth in hers and our black Topshop dresses were almost identical. Later, I saw her leaning into him in a way I didn't love. I'd been cornered by a drunk girl named Lindsay who told me all about her recent break-up, how she needed to get the fuck out of London. I told her she was lucky to have the choice, but she waved that away. 'He'll propose soon,' she said, looking over at Tom. 'You'll see.'

Next day, on the train home, he was quiet. Eventually he came out and said it—seeing Becca had been difficult, she had this power over him. 'I can't explain it,' he said. To me it didn't seem that hard to explain. I watched the repetitive countryside go by. The woman opposite was playing with her phone, obviously listening in.

'What would you say are the chances,' I finally said, 'of something happening that would mean I didn't have to leave in September?'

He looked at his hands. 'Leave me?' he said. 'Or leave London?'

The eyebrows of the woman opposite went up.

My first morning here I woke at eleven, confused. My animals had fallen out of bed. Downstairs I found my mother drinking coffee and circling items in an IKEA catalogue. She crossed a kitchen plank to fetch me a cup and we sat at the white plastic table. When I asked where my father was, she mumbled something dubious. Her coffee isn't what it was when I left.

She saw me taking in the state of the place. 'Not quite what you were expecting.' She fussed at a mark on the table. When I was younger, her make-up was always perfect—habit from flying, I guess. Now her fingernails are chewed and unpainted, eyebrows long overdue for a pluck.

Last year, she told me, my father had dozed off at the wheel and rear-ended a Mazda at a stoplight in midtown Sac—two shot tail-lights, nobody hurt. The other driver was a hefty woman in her forties who emerged from her vehicle in a bloodthirsty rage. Shaken, my father had pulled into the Wells Fargo on the corner, withdrawn a stack of bills and given them to the woman, who'd accepted them without comment.

A few weeks later, the summons had arrived. The woman had sued for the 'totalled' car and the aggravation of an old neck injury sustained a decade prior. CCTV from the ATM showed my father handing over the cash, unsteady on his feet, unmistakable in his favourite Hawaiian shirt. An attorney—Jiro Yamada was his name—advised them to settle. That, plus all the fees, meant they had to sell the house, which had lost a ton of value in the crash. They sold all the furniture too, save for one or two heirlooms and the stuff in my old room.

'We weren't bankrupt,' my mother said, 'but we were pretty damn close.'

Around this time, she went on, my father developed an obsession with chance, inspired mostly by a *Frontline* episode about math whizzes winning big at online poker. He began calculating the probability of the precise catastrophic sequence of events that had befallen him. First it was the odds of rear-ending that particular woman, based on the Greater Sacramento population. Then the odds of falling asleep at the wheel, which apparently afflicted one in four people at least once in their lifetime. Odds of picking Dos Señoritas of all local restaurants, odds of choosing that night of the week for a mosey downtown, of taking that particular route home. Then there was the previous night's disrupted sleep, which had affected alertness as well as inclination to excessive IPA consumption, which could in turn be blamed for the attempt to buy his way out of trouble. But what exactly had disrupted his sleep? And if you really got into it—decision to move to Sac from the Bay in '76, opening of Wells Fargo account in '83, purchase of distinctive Hawaiian shirt in '02, reluctance to destroy shirt after incident. On and on.

'Remember Dale?' my mother said, meaning my father's old college roommate. 'That's his place.' She gestured with her head at the other house. 'He's never there, of course. He and Halimah spend most of their time in Florida now. He was about to level this one when your father called. Said we were welcome to live in it rent-free in exchange for sprucing it up.'

'Couldn't you live in there?' I said, using the same head movement as her.

She sipped her coffee and shook her head. 'If it wasn't for Dale, who knows where we would've ended up.' She looked around at the disarray, the pencilled numbers on bare drywall. 'The idea was to work and patch it up gradually. But work's not so easy to find. And then we heard about the five-dollar buffet at the Golden Peak.' She laughed a sad little laugh and shook her head. 'You know, he won over four thousand dollars that first week. Kept saying, "That's our new kitchen! That's our new laminate floor!" That was nearly a year ago. Of course, these days he gets a free pass for the buffet. Nothing like a big meal and some nice wine to get you in the mood.'

I took my cup over the planks to the sink. 'I didn't need to hear any of this?'

They hadn't wanted me to worry, she said. 'I really thought you were settling over there. And then, once we knew you were coming back . . .'

'You figured I didn't need any more bad news.'

It seemed like she was finally about to ask what had happened with Tom. But then my father came in and kissed our cheeks, whistling some old Sinatra song I knew but couldn't quite name.

In the afternoons, when she takes a nap, I go out to walk in the woods. Wild turkeys, squirrels and sometimes a deer or two that bolt when I get too close. Yesterday I peered through the windows of the big house next door and looked at all the furniture and fittings. I saw framed photographs of Dale and Halimah, standing in front of notable sights from each of the seven continents.

Apparently, Dale made his money in arbitrage, some-thing I don't understand or ever want to. Halimah's new Cayenne is parked outside. The keys are in a drawer in my parents' kitchen, though I haven't seen them drive it yet.

Days my father comes home all chipper, he's honest about where he's been. It reminds me of when he'd come home from the office and lift me up on to his shoulders. On the other, far more frequent days, he hardly says a word. Sometimes he's out until the middle of the night and I hear him edge up the creaky stairs, see the beam of his headlamp flash for a second between my door and the floor.

Last night I called him at 1.30 a.m. to ask if he was okay.

'Nine hundred up on the night! That's a new table and chairs right there.'

'Is Gloria looking after you?'

'You know she is,' he said, like she was right there winking at him.

'Hey, Dad. I'm sorry about what happened. With the car and the house and everything.'

In the pause I heard background voices, the chorus of machines. 'Sometimes that's just how the cards fall, right, sweetie? Gotta play the hand you're dealt. Gotta take the consequences, intended or otherwise.'

The three of us should go to Calistoga tomorrow, I said, to the Petrified Forest, for old times' sake. There was another pause and I could tell he was troubled by the thought of being so far from the Golden Peak. But in the end he said sure, whatever you want.

After we hung up, I lay awake. At 2.15 a.m. I got up and got dressed and grabbed the Cayenne keys from the drawer. Soon I was walking in under the big flashing sign depicting mountains made out of glinting coins. I roamed until I came across his lucky machine. He wasn't there and no one was playing, so I dug out my gaming card and began hitting buttons at random. Soon I was up twenty-six dollars and could feel myself getting on a roll. Lemons, stars, eight balls—I willed some to stay, some to go. My winnings climbed to sixty-two bucks. I could hear my mother saying *Cash out!* I was up nearly a hundred before I started to lose. I felt my eyes widen, tongue loose in my open mouth, breath short—something rightfully mine was slipping away. The numbers kept falling as I hit the buttons, harder and harder, one little win and I'd be back on track. But the machine had turned against me. It leaked its sinister electronic cackle as the zeros began to flash.

Across the restaurant I saw my father, alone at a table set for a dozen, plates before him stacked with untouched food, staring at his reflection or else out into the night.

This morning, I found them at the plastic table. My father's head hung, his hands were clasped. My mother had ripped out a catalogue page and was tearing the page into tiny pieces.

We drove down out of the drought-brown hills, around Sac, across the valley and up past Napa. The sky was blue but the vines were all bare, and the sticks in their rows looked like crosses in a military cemetery. We listened to NPR and didn't really speak. My father slept in the back, hands in his lap like a nervous child. My mother drove erratically, hunched at the wheel. The radio talked about high-school gangs in Chicago, how there's no safe way for kids to walk home—alone means threatened, together means a threat.

Past Calistoga we turned up into the forested hills, went over a peak and descended again, sunlight cascading through the trees on to the windshield and catching on finger marks. When we pulled into the gravel parking lot, my father looked around like we'd kidnapped him.

The visitors' centre was smaller than I remembered, but the geodes and shark's teeth in matrix seemed the same. The old man at the desk, who had sepia teeth and grey hair parted neatly, said ten dollars each to get on the trail. My mother paid. I took a leaflet from the rack and we set out anti-clockwise as instructed, the two of them close behind me. My legs felt shaky, eyes raw from lack of sleep. Everything was quiet.

I heard my mother mutter something barbed and a few paces later my father muttered back. I opened up the leaflet and began to read aloud in my best British tour-guide voice.

'Over three million years ago, a volcano erupted seven miles north-east of here and a tremendous earthquake shook the country.'

My mother said something I didn't quite catch, something like we can't go on like this.

'The pale yellow sandy ash that resulted is the soil you walk on today.'

My father either told her she was being dramatic or else that she was mean and pathetic.

'Fire, ash and molten lava coursed down the valley in which now stands the Petrified Forest.'

We passed what the leaflet called the Pine Pit Tree, two feet in diameter, forty-three feet in length exposed. This too was smaller than I remembered but no less strange.

'I mean it,' my mother said, her voice cracking. 'It has to stop.'

'Water laden with silicates in the ash seeped down into the gaps left behind by the decomposing tree fibres, replacing the wood cell by cell with crystallized silica until the entire tree became stone.'

We passed the Giant, sixty feet in length, six feet in diameter. My father raised his voice. 'You tell her what really went on? Tell her about you and that asshole Yamada?'

My mother sobbed once and gathered herself immediately, as if we'd hit a pocket of turbulence. 'You promised.'

'Yeah, well. People make promises all the time.'

We came to the Queen of the Forest. Eight feet in diameter, sixty-five feet in length exposed. It lay there, immense and terrible somehow, like the full-scale blue whale replica at the Natural History Museum, like a fallen pillar in an Ancient Greek ruin. Every detail of what had once been wood—every texture and grain of the bark— was present, lifelike, but stone dead. It was the ghost of the tree, a monument to it.

'An ocean covered this area more than once during the last three hundred million years.' I could hear my voice faltering. 'Fossilized fish and shells have been found with petrified snails and clams.'

At the end, Tom came out to Heathrow on the train, lugging my suitcases up and down stairs. We sat outside a Pret on the metal chairs, splitting an orange juice, not meeting each other's eyes. Numerous things remained to be said but the time for saying them had passed. I leaned across the table and kissed him on the forehead and spilled what was left of the juice.

Leaving them standing silently apart, I went up on to the little viewing platform. The autumnal canopy was dense and cool. A couple came slowly up the trail toward us, a frail man in a wheelchair pushed by a woman. They looked to be seventy or sixty-five and the woman leaned into her task, breathing hard. The wheels sank into the ashy soil and they came to a halt. My parents went over to lend a hand, helping the woman manoeuvre the chair back on to firmer ground. The man's face gave nothing away.

My parents joined me on the bench, one on each side. I curled up, feet in my father's lap, head in my mother's. I wanted someone to tell me how things will turn out, or if not how then why. But I guess I'm too old to be thinking like that. She stroked my hair, tapped twice on the leaflet, like back when she would help me with homework and my mind would start to drift.

'Fossilized fish,' she said, to show she'd been listening, remind me how far I'd got. 'Petrified snails.'

9. The Unstables

There it goes, climbing skyward, plane containing son. Third of three to leave her, one way or another. Her forehead leaves a greasy mark on the car window. Maybe she imagines it but the wings seem to actually flutter. She pictures Tom up there, shifting in his seat, swallowing as the landscape falls away. She hates that moment when the gear folds up, the mechanical groan and clunk of it. She cranes her neck, twists, strains against the seatbelt, but what's the use, he's gone. Third of three.

Lucy sits back. Clear, warm September day, no fog, no delays. Is she supposed to be grateful?

From the radio, suddenly, that 'Firestarter' song. Again? *Still?* 'Song' is a stretch, honestly. Was there something equivalent when she was eighteen? A hit that ticked every box for her but sounded to her mother like industrial waste? The Stones never had devil-horn hair like that. Though, now she thinks about it, didn't Terry drive them all mad at uni playing Pink Floyd records backwards, revealing Satanic messages and such? Oh, Terry. Always such a character.

Roger turns it all the way down.

'I was enjoying that,' she says. It made her think of Tom, in fact, who'd played it relentlessly in his room back when it had first come out, a couple of years before. Not that she needs any prompting to think of her airborne son.

Roger looks over briefly, drives them towards the airport exit in silence. His window whirrs open and the machine to which he feeds the plastic card seems to offer a kind of response. The barrier lifts, another whirr. Are they communicating with one another, these contraptions? Talking about her? Exchanging snide remarks about her husband's teeth?

Steady on, Luce.

At the Forest Road junction, he slows to a halt, though stopping's not required, peering as if lost in each direction before accelerating gently. Why so gently? Drive normally, please.

Back to work, then—museum for her, office for him. An hour away to wave Tom off, now back to see out this Tuesday afternoon as if no blow has been absorbed, no hollowing sustained. But home appeals even less. Hangers in his wardrobe still clanging. It'll be days before she can strip his bed, remove the glass of dusty water, tidy and straighten. But that's what you do, isn't it? Tidy, straighten, hoover, dust.

No, going home does not appeal. At least at work there's the computer and hopefully a new message on it from Terry.

Roger shifts into third and his hand moves on until it rests on her knee. Odd gesture, that. He pats her twice. The hand lingers. She feels him glance across.

'I gave him twenty quid for the train,' he says.

She nods. Wants to move her leg so the hand will fall away. 'Is that enough?'

Hand returns to wheel.

In the check-in queue, Tom lugging his suitcase and backpack forward two feet at a time, she chattered away like an idiot, grabbing things at random from her spiralling brain—they've been forecasting fog but they're wrong again, funny how Americans call university 'school', wonder what your room will be like, the Hyde Park in Leeds is much smaller than London's, I'll get you those tickets for Millennium Eve the minute they go on sale, it'll be here before you know it.

'Don't you want a coffee or something, Mum?'

Other kids were heading off too, kids whose parents had dropped them at the entrance. Roger took her arm and led her towards the poky café. 'Let go of me,' she snarled, under her breath, just as they were passing the De Lisle woman. What was her name? Something boyish like Andie or Sam. Immaculate as always, make-up and hair, must be nice to be loaded, at your permanent leisure. Lucy felt Roger's eyes widen as he did as he was told. 'Posh cow,' she said, not particularly quietly, as they joined the café queue and watched the Latvian lad wrestle with the ancient espresso machine. 'Where does she think she is, Chelsea bloody Flower Show?'

'*Shush*, for God's sake.'

'Oh, shut up yourself.'

As they sat there with their lattes, waiting for Tom to join them, to come and say goodbye, it crossed her mind to march over to the desk and buy herself a ticket. One way, please. No bag, no. Window would be fine, thanks. See him to his room, get him settled, get the necessities in from ASDA or Tesco, loo roll, Weetabix, Tetley, milk. And then, what?

On TV the other week, that woman who really did it. Belinda Ellis. Regular person, not a celeb, only on the box because of what she'd done. Which was: vanish. Fifty-two she was, older than Lucy but not by much. Husband, four kids, one still at home, a girl, a goth. Decent job at an ophthalmologist's. Thetford, that was the town. Not far from Norwich. Extensive planning, they reckoned. Years of careful preparation. Left for work one morning, never seen again, silver Ford Focus found parallel-parked on the road behind the station. That was it. No CCTV trace, no transactions, no sightings. Total sublimation. 'It's hard to fathom,' Mr Ellis said, near the end of the documentary. There were hairs creeping out of his nostrils that Lucy had to assume Belinda used to keep in check. 'It's hard to come to terms.'

No sleep that night, or barely. Not plotting or anything so wild as that. Marvelling at the sheer audacity. Marvelling and actually fearing slightly the excitement in her chest.

She'd been hearing things, Belinda Ellis—so the husband said. Words and phrases concealed in noise. That had been all he could think of when the detectives asked him for tell-tale signs, ominous behaviour, clues. 'She thought things were speaking to her,' he said. 'Birds, dishwashers, lawnmowers.' What did they say? Different stuff, the husband said. Nonsense, rubbish. It was obvious he didn't want to say. Can you give us an example? He sighed, the husband, rubbed his face. '*Dreamy treehouse*, that was one. She said the carwash was telling her *dreamy treehouse.*' Had she seemed disturbed by this, the presenter wanted to know. Not disturbed, no, the husband said. Quite chuffed, actually.

On the right now, La Villette Garage—no carwash there. Off La Villette Lane, where Polly used to live. Lovely house, that one, enormous kitchen, two living rooms, TV in each. Hamilton Cottage, they called it, after the capital of Bermuda, where they'd lived for most of the eighties. Seemed extravagant at first, his and hers tellies. But then, later, essential.

Polly left too, of course. Not in the Belinda Ellis sense, but still. That was the problem with this wretched island. You made a friend, made the effort, then they buggered off back to the mainland to do up a farmhouse in Somerset, or else to Jersey or the Isle of Man, their husbands got transferred to the Geneva office, or their mothers up in Cumberland needed looking after once the second new hip went in. Look at Polly. Four years of friendship, coffees in Dix-Huit on a Saturday morning before a leisurely browse in Next or M&S, maybe Spinnaker if they were having a sale. Double-date dinners when the men could be persuaded. It was Polly who got her riding—riding! For a while, anyway. Sunday mornings at the stables near Sausmarez Manor. 'The unstables,' Polly called them, they were so old and rickety. Lucy never had the confidence Polly had, never felt comfy in all the get-up, the boots and jodhpurs and silly hats. But

Polly was so encouraging. She never pushed or pressured Lucy, helped her learn how to be with the horses, how to stay calm so that they did too. 'Off we go,' Polly always said, as they moved cautiously out into the cold field. It became a sort of joke, whenever they were leaving a shop or café. *Off we go, off we go!*

It took a few months, but she started to improve. First thing she'd been good at in years, though 'good' was a stretch. She grew attached to one horse in particular, a Cleveland Bay called Rude Boy. He had a long neck, wide, sloping shoulders and a bright white star between his eyes. She liked to stroke that star with her thumb. He was a moody sod who could go from calm to stroppy in a flash. No one else liked to ride him much, but that only made her fonder.

Occasionally she thought of asking Roger if he'd like to come and watch her one Sunday. But he never showed much interest, and actually, she realized one day, his being there—smirking, honing quips and jibes to needle her with later—would only ruin it.

Sometimes, during those months, on nights when Roger snored her awake, she lay in bed and thought about Rude Boy, less than a mile away in his stable. His unstable. Was he warm enough, she wondered. Was he awake too? Sometimes she imagined walking up there in the dark, through the quiet lanes in her dressing gown and slippers, to cosy up beside him on his bed of hay amid the creaking wood, feel the beating of his massive heart against her own ribs.

But then one day a car backfired as it passed the gate,

some stupid kid in a souped-up Golf, just as she and Rude Boy were getting up to a trot. She barely remembered it, honestly, the fall. But the moment of clarity right before, when she knew he was about to throw her—that she's never forgotten.

Not long after, Polly announced she was moving to Grand Cayman. Their housing licence wasn't being renewed. 'This island and its bloody rules,' she said. Lucy tried to be supportive—sounds like paradise, all of that. She tried not to feel sorry for herself. She was safe, she'd married a local. Her boys had never had to relocate, adapt to new schools, make new friends. They'd never had to start again as a family, learn a new place, its weather and rules, its shortcuts and teams and supermarkets, bus timetables, bin-collection days. No one had ever told her she had to leave. No one ever would.

Polly came around to say goodbye. Packing's a nightmare, these movers are morons, why does it all end up last minute? Roger was out, thank God. Lucy smiled and smiled, but soon enough she was blubbing, and when they hugged it was hard not to say, 'Can't I *come*?'

She could have kept going to the stables, of course. 'You can't be scared of horses, love!' Roger said. 'They don't mean you any harm. Go on, go back, give it another whirl.' But, whenever he would suggest it, Lucy would hear herself make up some excuse—the boys need help with their homework, I'm up to my elbows in ironing, rubbish like that. Her boots got steadily buried at the back of the cupboard under the stairs.

She hardly ever thinks about Rude Boy now.

Yes, that was Polly, gone just like that, like a space-ship came down and sucked her up. Like she'd been silently removed in the middle of the night. Abduction was never considered in the Belinda Ellis case, mainly because Belinda Ellis left a note. Not a suicide note but a couple of lines saying she was going away and don't try to find her. *There's chicken kievs in the freezer.* That was how she closed. Then two kisses and a single fold.

At that point in the documentary, Lucy glanced over at Roger. He was slumped in the brown leather arm-chair, dozing, chin tucked wetly into neck.

Not far from Polly's old place, hidden away in the lanes, the cemetery. Invisible from the main road but towering as ever, looming like a lighthouse with its beam trained on her all these years. Sometimes getting to it is stupidly hard, one car after another met on the narrow road, that pause when you each hope the other will do the honours, reversing or tucking up against the grassy bank to make enough room to squeeze through.

But it's always peaceful, the cemetery. Restful. More than once she's lain out in the sun and snoozed for fif-teen or twenty minutes. No harm in it. *Gone to the mansions of rest.* That's what it says on her grandfather's headstone, in the graveyard out near Beeston, hundreds of miles away from here. She was six and three quarters when he died—someone at the funeral asked her, no recollection now of who but giving that precise answer she remem-bers very clearly. Wanting to say seven but not wanting to lie. The mansions were opulent but comfy in her mind, with plush red carpets and big high windows, white light sloshing in.

When her first baby died, Lucy thought of that line on Granddad's stone. When decisions needed making, impossible decisions. It didn't seem quite right. The image of her little girl alone forever in some stuffy dusty room with the silverware untouched, cooing unheeded on some lost upper floor of a huge, silent house—no. Rest for a tired old man, fine. Not for a child who never even sat up. Who never even learned to swing her tiny arm and roll.

In the end they put her name and the dates.

When the boys were small, they went as a family, every year on Imogen's birthday, 25 September. It felt like the right thing to do, even if the boys seemed unsure how to act. One time, she remembers now, a Lennon song came on the radio as they drove. As they pottered about the grave in the late-summer sunlight, she watched Tom, four or five years old, lean in close to the headstone and whisper, barely loud enough for Lucy to hear, 'Imogen, there's no heaven!' She turned to Roger to see if he'd heard too, but no. I'll tell him about it later, she thought, knowing it would make him smile. She didn't, though. She kept it to herself, tucked it away like a bone-smooth piece of bottle-green sea glass you found on a wintry beach as a child and slipped under your pillow.

The family visits tailed off. And Roger stopped going years ago, as far as she knows. Not that she exactly blames him for that. At some point she stopped mentioning her own visits, and even that she didn't especially mind—going alone suited her, and the intimacy of it was heightened by the secrecy. But all those things together, all those evasions, added up to what felt to her like a kind of failure. Failure to honour the loss, to carry it between them, one at each end, instead of each of them dragging their own.

Hard on the boys too, she's always felt. A sister left behind before they even came along. She's seen the way they are, always pining for something they'll never have or someone they haven't yet found. The thought of some distant, absent figure. The idea of an echo, an answer, sent back. Or was it only in her, that feeling? Was she only—what did they call it—*projecting*? Polly would know.

Ah, Polly.

Roger turns right on to the main road through St Martin's, twenty-odd years on the island now and she still couldn't tell you what this road is called. Past the post office and the hardware shop and the Co-op, where once, years ago, she sliced the tip off one of Ned's fingers. How old would he have been, eighteen months? Her mind was scattered, where was her list, the simplest of tasks a baffling struggle with the grappling child in her arms. To get him in the seat, simply to get him in the seat was incomprehensibly difficult. Shoppers pushing past her, the wail in her ears, she's never been able to remember exactly but she steadied the trolley with her foot and reached for the seat bar, still holding him, folded it down and the next thing she knew he was screaming, long pauses in between where he sucked in breath, seemingly astonished at the pain, the blood spurting out of the abbreviated finger, crude and shockingly hot.

She stood there in the fruit and veg aisle, the little hand deep in her mouth, pressing his howling face into her throat, sucking, tasting the blood, thinking second of two, second of two. Thinking if she was going to lose this one too, the least she could do was swallow all the blood so he wouldn't have to see it pooling on the floor.

Though, actually, it was Tom who turned out squeamish, not Ned. Tom who nipped his thumb once and fainted when he saw the red drops leaking out. 'That knife's too sharp for a youngster like me,' he said, once he recovered. She's always remembered that. Oh, did they laugh.

Something occurs to her. 'Did he pack any cutlery?'

Roger smiles in a way that makes her want to tear off his nearest ear. 'They have that kind of thing over there, you know. Plates too, I think. Bowls, pans. Besides, he'll be living on takeaway pizza.'

'He'd better bloody not.'

He looks at her again and she ignores him. She's thinking of Tom, how he would come into the kitchen and offer to lay the table. Even long after it had become routine, still he would ask, 'Shall I lay the table, Mum?' Part of it was wanting credit, she thought, wanting the gesture acknowledged. But her thanks never seemed to register, never prompted a response. So maybe it was only that he liked the routine, depended on it. This became more evident when, one day, she noticed—he was twelve or thirteen—that he was giving himself the same fork every time.

The cutlery drawer has always been a mess, their collection pulled together from various sets over the years. Wooden handles, plastic handles, pure metal. Rounded ends, squared ends. One fork in particular is distinct. It belongs to no set they have ever owned, its origins a mystery. Pinched from a restaurant? Left behind by dinner guests who'd brought it in their homemade coleslaw or something? Or maybe picked up at a car-boot or jumble, fivepence, tenpence, a solitary fork, unremarkable to the naked eye, smooth navy plastic casing on the handle with a hole at the tip as if to hang from a rack, a rack she has never seen. Every meal, every night, he laid it at his place. A week or so after observing this, she laid the table herself, leaving that particular fork in the drawer.

He came in as usual when *Neighbours* ended, the six o'clock news theme booming dramatically down the hall. 'Shall I—oh.'

She busied herself at the stove. 'All done, thanks, lovey.' She stirred the Bolognese and waited. He mooched around the kitchen, touching things, taking an old cleaned-up Nutella jar from the cupboard and filling it with tap water, taking a swig. She was grinning, sure that he could see it from behind, the slight lift of her ears, the widening of her jaw. The anticipation was delicious, the subterfuge. Finally, she heard the drawer slide open, the metallic note of something removed. She imagined him slipping it up inside his shirt, the sleeve of his white school shirt with blue spots of flicked ink strewn up the back (it was a prank at school, he'd told her when she'd caught him in his room with an ink eraser, hunched like some scholar over an ancient manuscript, patiently blotting each little spot—everyone does it to everyone, not just me—oh, her heart!). The urge to turn and look was strong, but she resisted, kept stirring. He did something at the table, returned to the drawer, placed something in it delicately, closed it almost silently.

That night, in bed, she mentioned it to Roger.

'Little nutter.' He was still leafing through Sunday's *Times* five days later. 'Though to be fair I've been known to raise a stink at work when my mug's not been in the cupboard.'

'It's not the fork itself that worries me. It's the attachment. The fixation.'

'Hide it. Chuck it out. Where did it come from, anyway?' He turned the page laboriously, folded the paper. 'What's Clarkson saying now, then.'

Check the drawer later, she thinks, now, as they pass the Chinese from where they've picked up takeaways fortnightly for fifteen-plus years. If he's taken it, he'll be fine.

'What did he say was his email address?' Roger says.

They pass the unstables. How old must Rude Boy be by now? She doesn't try to look. Probably wouldn't see much anyway, not with the two high granite walls on either side of the gravel driveway. On round the corner, past Sausmarez Manor, with its croquet lawn and miniature train that she took the boys to ride on when they were small. Ned fell off, she remembers, trying to ride standing up.

'It's by the phone,' she says. 'GreekGifts at something.'

'You'll be needing one yourself, then. Don't imagine we'll be getting many letters. Or phone calls, for that matter.'

She's had one for months, of course. Needed it to sign up for Friends Reunited, which was how she found Terry. Didn't recognize his face in the photo to begin with, bald and bearded, but on closer inspection there were traces of the sexy Terry she'd known, what—thirty years ago? Three years divorced now, his own chiropractic practice, a daughter doing history at Warwick. Their messages started off innocently enough. But after a few weeks of covertly tapping them out at the shared computer in the museum's musty office, she noticed him getting bolder. Was she happy? Had she thought about him over the years? Did she remember that night at his parents' house, when the two of them had jumped in the pool? *Vaguely*, she wrote, though in truth the memory is still so strong it almost takes her breath, like she's plunging again into that chilly water, naked, tipsy, full of young life. She remembers the dark sky, the dew-jewelled grass, and looking at Terry, thinking she would do anything, not in a sex way but in the sense that she was suddenly, electrically, wide awake. When he peeled off his clothes and dived in, she stood there alone for a couple of seconds, watching him climb through the light of the pool. She remembers screaming at the knife-like cold and, when she surfaced and turned, seeing him standing with arms spread like wings, skin all licked with wet light. She was screaming, gasping, while he shouted and shouted that this must be it, the moment of perfection that nothing would beat.

I was right, he wrote, the other day. *Nothing did.*

Did Belinda Ellis run off for love? The question was posed near the end of the documentary, by which time Roger, in the armchair, was snoring full-tilt. The husband thought not. Lucy is inclined to agree with him, but still not totally convinced. Was leaving to be with someone else worse than leaving to be alone? Or was it better, more forgivable?

They are no longer moving. They've come to a halt on Fort Road, approaching the top of the Val des Terres, though not close enough yet to look down on the harbour and out across to Jethou, Herm and the other islands. Slipping the stick into neutral, Roger pulls up the handbrake. This strikes her as excessive, a sort of brag that he has intuitively understood this delay will be significant. She sees, stretching ahead, a line of cars, but no sign of what's causing the jam. No oncoming traffic, she notices, which seems to suggest—something.

'What's all this, then,' he says.

A couple of people have got out of their cars but have gone no further and stand with hands to their foreheads, shielding from the sun. No one is shouting or sounding their horns. This is good, she understands, a sign of decorum. Still, it infuriates her. The rage is unexpected, exciting. Must they all sit here and take it? Blow your horns, she thinks. Blow your bloody horns, make a scene, raise hell.

A woman looks back at their car and beyond, and

Lucy understands that the queue now goes on behind them, more cars joining it every few seconds, everyone dutifully falling into line, as if spinning around to find another route would be indecent, an act of aggression.

They sit without speaking, the engine turning over. It's warm inside the car with no breeze blowing through, so she lowers her window. Air flows in. A sharp noise reaches her, a guttural shriek, but before she can consider its source there is a man at the window on the driver's side, plump face drizzled with sweat, eyes behind sunglasses.

'Afternoon,' the man says. 'Anyone any good with a horse?'

She watches her husband. His hands are on the wheel. She can't see his face because it's turned to the window, but she knows that his eyebrows are raised.

'What's it doing on a main road?' he says.

'Indeed,' says the man, already moving on to the car behind.

Lucy looks across at Roger. He stares straight ahead, tongue probing in the inside of his cheek. She can see that it has occurred to him to suggest she go and help. But to do so would give away his own fear, the same fear he has mocked in her. She can see him trying to decide what to do. She has a sudden urge to tell him all about Terry. Not her feelings for him now or even back then, long before she and Roger ever met, before she'd ever heard of Guernsey. No, she wants to *describe* Terry—his large ears, the Floyd obsession, his tendency to start a new paragraph after every sentence in his messages on the computer. She wants to bore him senseless about Terry, smother him in details of the other man's life until he finally understands.

'I suppose I could have a look,' he says.

'Go on, then.'

The door slams and he moves off reluctantly, rolling up his sleeves as he goes. The man in the sunglasses trots to catch up. Alone, a new absence locates her, coiling around her from behind her seat. Again, she hears the shriek, more clearly this time. This time, she recognizes it. Or, rather, she knows its source. And without a thought, she echoes it. Screws her eyes shut and shrieks back in kind, as loud and for as long as she can.

The man in the sunglasses turns to look back, but she doesn't see that.

The thing that really got her about Belinda Ellis—the thing that kept her awake that night—wasn't that she'd disappeared. It was that she'd disappeared so perfectly, so beautifully, and ended up famous for it. Vanished by her own impeccable design, only to be beamed into millions of homes, only to be judged and discussed by strangers, her motives dissected, her decisions picked over and pecked apart by all those prying beaks. And of course it had been in the papers too. Radio, Internet. She was nowhere, she was gone, but she was everywhere.

Was she watching from afar, furious in her treehouse? Cursing her hopeless husband, wishing he'd trimmed his nostril forest before the camera crew arrived? No. Better to imagine her beyond it all, reclining somewhere by a glinting pool in Mexico or Brazil, trade winds swishing through high palm fronds, telling her whatever she chose to hear. Icy Daiquiri in hand, warm sun on her anonymous face.

Lucy opens her eyes.

Movement, now, up ahead. Dark brown with that little splash of white, a blur of sinew, hair, tooth. She feels her breath catch in her throat. He is clattering towards her, pounding and mad. She watches him come. She sees only the horse, not the scattering people, not the stationary cars. As he passes, their eyes meet, ever so briefly, through the portal of the open window. It's an instant, no more, the slightest flicker, but she's certain he sees her, her stroppy beast.

His hooves beat the tarmac in a steady rhythm but louder somehow is the sound of his breathing, the vast lungs filling and emptying out in frantic, sawing rasps. She listens intently to the drumming hooves, the thundering breaths. The two horse noises are all she can hear. And as Rude Boy gallops away behind, three words emerge from beneath or between them, as clear as if bellowed straight into her ear. *Off we go*, say the hooves and heaving lungs. *Off we go, off we go.*

10. Brazil and Back

One fire after another. That's how I remember that summer. Every time they'd put one out, the next would go from a couple sparks to full-blown inferno in an afternoon. The drought was a few years old by then, so nothing needed much persuading to burn. The names weren't people's names, not like with storms. Butte Fire, Rocky Fire, Valley Fire. Fork Complex, Mad River Complex. When you hear complex you know those guys have their hands full. Smoke hung and drifted in the air. First thing you smelled in the morning, last thing you smelled at night. Even on the news they seemed nervous. Five per cent contained, they said. Ten per cent, seven per cent. Cause unknown, they said. Mandatory evacuations.

One day, I asked Sean what *contained* meant. Anything to get him talking. He'd been home a couple months by then. On the sofa, Raiders sweatpants, pale, clammy, scruffy beard, not shaky exactly but not steady either. It was eleven in the morning and I was still in my PJs. As far as I could tell, he hadn't been to bed. Hadn't moved, in fact, since I got in from work, except maybe to pee and grab snacks.

'Blocked off, I guess,' he said, eyes on the screen. Two nights later, I'd get the call from Folsom PD, telling me where he was.

'Out? Like they've put ten per cent of it out?'

He changed the channel to *Tree Fu Tom*, some kids' thing he was way too into then. 'More like that much can't go any farther.'

'So it's still burning as bad? But not moving so fast.'

He made an impatient sound. Then he scratched his head like it was urgent, behind the left ear, for way longer than you'd need for a regular itch. 'You get bit or something?' I said.

He didn't hear me. 'It means it's still kicking their asses,' he said.

He shifted, grimacing, which meant his hip was starting to hurt again where the bullets went in. I watched him dig the little plastic bottle from his pocket, shake out two pills. As he swallowed them, he held it up to count. Four left.

'We've got bug spray, you know.' I got up to go take a shower. 'Help yourself.'

First time I put the feelers out, I'll admit, I was nervous. Ask the wrong dude and word goes straight upstairs to Arturo. Zero tolerance, he always said. And since everything tanked and the foreclosure wolves started sniffing around, keeping that job was more important than ever. But I figured I'd never had so much as a warning. Plus, customers loved me. I had regulars blowing 5K a week, more, on the roulette wheels and poker tables. Besides, there's no law against *enquiring*, right? And I could always say they weren't for me.

It was 2 a.m. and my shift was finally done. One of my

regs had been in with his family. The daughter, Maggie, had gotten engaged and they were having a little celebration. Nice British boy. He'd flown out, gone down on one in the SFO baggage claim—the whole nine. They'd been broken up, was my understanding. Poor kid looked terrified. Watching whatever fire was in the distance like it was coming straight for him. But who hasn't felt like that at one time or another?

As I was waving them off—Maggie and her new fiancé held each other on the escalator, I noticed—another familiar face rolled in with three fishing buddies. 'Gloria,' Gabe said, 'these gentlemen wish to feast like kings and be waited on by a princess.' So that kept me busy. After midnight it got quieter, so I leaned into the kitchen to cosy up to some slicers and dicers. Half were illegals anyway, so I figured I was safe. Plus the testosterone in there was so thick you could scrape it off the ceiling with a squeegee—I only had to squeeze a bicep or two and they were lining up to give me the lowdown. One, sweet little guy with a wispy goatee, offered to escort me right up to Vivian's spot. *Después*, he said, nodding at his boss. I know Viv, I told him. Or thought I did.

Viv had been around then what, four years? She had a son too, thirteen or so. Has. Older by now, I guess. These days she doesn't ask about Sean, and when I tell her anyway she gets this look on her face like *someone put this poor bitch out of it*. But she still gives me what I ask for.

I let her deliver a tray of beers and grab her purse, then followed her past the slots and roulette tables into the restrooms in the far corner, over by the shitty old machines that no one played. She peed and then we had to wait for this haggard old crone to finish farting and sighing and washing her hands like they were caked in her husband's dried blood. Once she'd shuffled out, I told Viv what I was hunting.

'Perks?' she said. 'Sure, baby. Ankle still giving you heck?'

That was in reference to a night the previous year when I'd rolled clean off my left heel and torn some ligament or cartilage or other, not to mention taken a fresh plate of shrimp carbonara and smeared it all up and down some guy's plaid fleece shirt. I nodded. Viv produced the pills and took my money in a single smooth move. Twenty-five in a little Ziploc baggy. Actually she tucked them right in my bra and straightened me up like she was wiping my nose before she packed me off to school. 'You want stronger, I got stronger. Just holler, all right?'

I drove home with them right there against my chest. He needs it, I told myself, he needs it and they don't give him enough.

Sean was, like always, awake. When he'd first come home, he'd slept and slept, which later I discovered was a bad sign. Sixteen, eighteen hours a day. I'd taken the week off to settle him in, cook his favourites, do his laundry. Chicken chimichangas, pulled pork. Keep him company. That was one thing they warned us about. *An uncharacteristic inclination towards solitude.* Some other mother was all, *Isn't it all gonna be un-cara-tristic? Isn't that why we're here?*

But no one mentioned too much sleep, so I let him

wallow. I mean, how tired must these boys be? Here's us bitching about our memory foam being too hot or the neighbours cranking up their video games—meanwhile these kids are over there curled up in the desert knowing some little fucker is probably at that exact moment strapping explosives to the dog you just taught to catch a Frisbee.

That was one Sean told me, later, when I did get him talking a little.

The screaming had kicked in his third week back. I heard him from the driveway when I got home from work. By the time I got up there he was quiet again, out cold but crazy sweaty. And then I smelled it and it was like the last sixteen years hadn't happened and he was still six years old, trying to work the machine in the dark, trying not to wake me up, spilling detergent all over the floor, so mad and stubborn when I tried to help. Back then the paediatrician said it was his father walking out, the transition to life with an absent dad.

So this was another transition, I figured. A phase. But he screamed like that every night, till gradually the big sleeping wore off and he was barely getting any at all. Till you could see he was actually afraid to doze off and deliver his mind to the devil on a plate.

I found him in the hallway, at the computer, doing the usual. It hit me like a wave as I went by. That farmy smell—the one downside of his time at the ranch.

'Maybe a shower today, sweetie? What do you think?'

'I need fents,' he said. 'Those perks aren't doing shit.'

'What is that? Stronger?'

'Better is what it is. Fents or oxy. And don't just get me another little bag.'

'What did I tell you? What did we *agree*?'

His head did this rolling, rotating thing that first started up when he was small. *Fine, whatever, Mom, jeez.* Used to drive me crazy, but I loved to see it then. Showed me he was still in there somewhere. My bubba.

'You need more MiraLAX too?' I said.

'And Peeps. But only the yellow ones. The others all taste like ass.'

He was eating those things by the box. I told him no wonder you can't poop, eating junk like that. But he loved them. And, honestly, when I'd see him sitting there, little yellow marshmallow ducklings lined up along the arm of the couch like they were marching towards some beautiful pond—when I'd watch him pick each one up as if it was a real-life baby bird, I'd feel like maybe we were doing all right. Then he'd bite the head clean off, of course. But you've got to start somewhere.

'These for your boy, by any chance?' Viv said, that night. We were in the usual restroom. 'Don't see you limping, is all. Don't see you favouring.'

I'd been careful what I told people. Said he was back and left it at that. But someone always knows someone who knows. Plus, the local rag ran a story about what happened down in Folsom. *Wounded Vet Found Unconscious in Parking Lot.* Which of course had to feature some speculative crap about his getting sent home and the reasons why. Thanks a bunch, jerkoffs. Sean never saw it as far as I know, but he probably had a feeling.

'He'll only go someplace else,' I said.

She nodded. 'You got MiraLAX?'

Once the deal was done, she leaned into the mirror and worked on her eyeshadow with a thumb.

'Pretty colour,' I said.

'Fire sapphire, they call it. Man, do they think up some stupid-ass names. So where was he at?'

I gave her the rundown. Two clean tours, then the third. The one that put a few chunks of metal in his butt and sent it home in a hurry.

'Bryce, my second cousin, is over there right now,' she said. 'His mom hasn't slept for months. Third cousin, excuse me. She cancelled her cable to stop herself sitting there watching the news go around.'

I nodded. I didn't tell her that I'd never really worried about Sean. I trusted that he was smart and tough enough to get out of there unharmed. I'm not superstitious, but my first thought when they told me what had happened was, *Gloria, you dummy, if you'd only worried some . . .*

'He seeing a shrink or whatnot?'

We were walking back out on to the floor, past the neglected machines. I told her, not unless you count Calvin and Hobbes.

'Oh my God, I love those two! My grandpa used to cut the strips out of the Sunday paper for me. They'll cheer you up no matter what.'

I was about to explain—I guess buying drugs off someone inclines you to give them your entire life story—but then a guy waved an empty glass in her direction and she gave me a *Back to the shitshow!* kind of look.

Jim and ginger. Flirty smile. Whatever people need to survive another night.

It was on the drive back from the hospital that he saw them. I was taking the scenic route, Green Valley Road up near Folsom Lake—what was left of it. Through El Dorado Hills, all the gold-brown fields. I had it in my head that seeing some countryside would do him some good. More good than the 50 at rush hour, anyway.

I'd planned a little speech. Planned to tell him that I'd never had time for any parenting book. Too busy working, trying to keep his father from putting another fist through the drywall. But sometimes I'd picked up tricks from other moms. For example, at the playground one day I'd watched this woman go through a little routine with her daughter. 'Five minutes,' she said, then 'Two minutes', then 'One minute'. Finally, it was 'Okay, pumpkin, do your last thing.' I'd always had a hell of a time getting Sean away from there, so I tried this woman's system. Counted down the minutes, then 'Do your last thing.' Worked like a charm. His last thing turned out to be going around saying bye-bye to all the other kids, even the ones he hadn't been playing with. Like he was leaving town for good and wanted them all to remember him.

That was what I wanted to tell him—don't let your last thing be something shitty like this.

But when it came down to it and I saw him there, waiting in the lobby at the VAMC, I suddenly had nothing to say. I just hugged him and kissed his beardy cheek for longer, I guess, than he felt was necessary.

'Okay, Mom,' he said. 'Okay, all right.'

So we were passing this place, an animal sanctuary, horses mostly but donkeys too, mules, goats, a few mutts. Prisha, one of the girls at the Peak, used to volunteer there, shovelling shit, raking hay. There were some sorry-looking horses in that field, tied up to poles, moping, wondering how'd I end up here, what happened to all the galloping and whatnot.

Suddenly, Sean was sitting up and acting all—I won't say *animated*, but definitely more *interested* than I'd seen him since back before he first shipped out. 'No way,' he said, twisting in his seat. 'Awesome.'

'What is it, bud? Horses?'

'Llamas.'

'Llamas?'

'Two llamas hanging out. Way over on the far side.'

The road curved and he eventually quit trying to look back. The VA doctor had told me she'd keep filling his prescription but only at the 'appropriate time'. I told her, Sean's idea of appropriate might be a little different than yours. She smiled at that, which was when I lost my cool, telling her he'll only go looking elsewhere, which is how he ended up unconscious outside Safeway in the first place—slumped against the wheel, honking the horn with his face, which the cops said probably saved his life given that people were banging on the window in thirty seconds flat—which is how this whole goddamn *inconvenience* came about.

She'd kept on smiling, heading for the door, applying sanitizer from a dispenser on the wall.

'You like llamas now?' I said.

'There was one in *Napoleon Dynamite*. That llama was sick. Shit, what was that llama's name.'

'What is that, a show?'

'Tory's favourite movie, like, ever. She made me watch it literally twenty-five times. Jesus, I can't believe I forgot.'

High-school sweethearts, those two. Good kids. Not angels, granted, but what kids that age are? She calmed him down. She got him away from a bad group of boys, not one of which, I might add, called to see how he was doing after he shipped back home. To her credit, she stuck by him for the first tour, but midway through the second I guess she'd had enough of getting her kicks from a vibrator and crying herself to sleep. Which I get. But Sean took it hard. Started asking more about her than me when he called. *Go see her for me. Tell her I love her.* I never went, not even when I told him I did.

I always liked Tory, though. She could take a joke. One morning she came in the kitchen in one of Sean's old T-shirts and not a lot else. 'I hope the earth moved for you, sweetie,' I said, 'because the house sure did.' I thought she might blush, but she just laughed, once. *Ha!* After that it seemed like they tried to keep it down. Still, I heard them one night on my way to the bathroom.

Panting and saying their sweet things. 'Seany, Seany, Seany,' she was whispering, 'we're on a sailboat, we're on a sailboat.' I lingered for a minute, leaning in. I can't say exactly what it felt like to hear them, but it didn't feel bad.

When we got back to the house, the first thing he did was look up that name.

'Fucking Tina!' I was in the kitchen, fixing him a sandwich I knew he wouldn't eat. He came in, yelling in a goofy voice, roaming around the kitchen, gesturing at someone or something that wasn't there. *'Tina, you fat lard, come get some dinner. Tina, EAT!'* He lunged at me and I flinched. I couldn't help it. *'Eat the food! Eat the food!'*

Was he crazy, I wondered, or excited? And what was the difference?

I put the sandwich on a plate and pushed the plate across the counter towards him. He slid it back and loped away, limping, I guess trying to walk like a llama.

'They can always use the help,' Prisha said. 'These flaky college kids show up once or twice and then get tired of the drive up from Sac. That or the shit-smell gets to them.'

We were in the break room, sharing the usual bag of peanut M&Ms. Prisha'd had a little stroke a few years back and her face was draggy on one side. It wasn't a bad look, actually. Dignified. Never let it get her down either. On the bright side, she told me not long after it happened, Ron's quit bugging me for oral pleasure.

'So he can show up whenever or what,' I said, throwing a couple candies in my mouth.

'Murray'll fix him up. He can be a hard-ass, honestly. But a man like Sean—well. He'll be fine.'

'Will he let him hang out with the llamas?'

'Can't see why not, if that's his thing.'

I wasn't crazy about the way she said that. But I also wasn't too dumb to know how the question sounded.

Three M&Ms left. Prisha took one and held the last two out—the opposite of what she would normally do. The side of her face that still moved assumed a sympathetic look.

Later that night, I asked Viv if she ever thought about what her life was adding up to. Can't remember why. Maybe it was all those old folks playing the slots, passing time until the coins ran out. It does something to you, seeing that same shit night after night. Did to me, anyway.

'What it's worth, you mean?' she said. We were in the restroom again. She looked tired. Tired but not unhappy. My cash was tucked inside her bra and her pills were tucked inside mine.

'Like if the things you're doing—or the things you've done so far, at least—if they add up, y'know? If they add up to *enough*.'

She chewed her gum and tilted her head like she was listening for something far off. I wondered what her eyeshadow was named.

'My uncle Tish tells a story,' she said. 'I mean, I must've heard this thing a hundred times. Worked his whole life at a bicycle store over in Auburn. Part time in high school, full time after. Ten years later he was managing the place, and by fifty he owned it outright. But then things got tight. People weren't buying so many bikes. Not from him, anyway. Rent goes up, all that. Right before he closes it down, he has a big sale to clear it all out. And on the very last day this guy moseys in. Old guy. Older than Tish, anyhow. "My God, is it you?" the guy says. Turns out, back in 1967 or whenever, little high schooler Tishy helped him pick out a bike. Told him, "This thing's so darn reliable, you could ride it to Brazil and back." Something goofy, y'know, making a sale. But that's exactly what this guy did.'

'Rode a bicycle to Brazil?'

'I guess he was drifting when he got out of school and the idea got stuck in his head. So he spent a couple years getting down there to Rio or wherever, and then eventually turned around and started heading back. But somewhere along the way—Guatemala, I believe—he met a girl and wound up staying. Village by the ocean, house on the beach. Got married, got a job, raised some little Guatemalan kids, the whole shebang. And now his wife had passed and he was back in California, first time in thirty-five years. And he says to Tish, "If it weren't for you, I shudder to think."'

'Let me guess,' I said. 'Millionaire. Bought all the bikes, saved the business.'

'Hell, no. Tish lost the store, sure enough. Lost his house, wound up crashing at my grandma's for a while. But he still tells that story every chance he gets.'

It was a nice story, I had to admit. But when I tried to imagine telling it to Sean, I couldn't see him listening. Or listening, maybe, but not hearing. Or else wondering what the hell kind of a name is Tish.

Next day, on my way to the Peak, I stopped by the ranch. You had to turn across the traffic, right on a blind corner, which seemed like a mistake on somebody's part. Up a long dirt track, dust billowing behind. Box elders made shade, and a few goats watched from the other side of some old wire fencing. Eventually you got to the little clearing where people parked. Chickens pecked around in the dirt, keeping half an eye on the dozen kitties lounging high and low in shade or sun. Orange kitties, black, white, tabby. A big grey thing with half a tail raised an eyelid as I climbed out of my CR-V. I could feel dust attaching to my legs.

There were four or five vehicles but no visible people. I could smell the animals, their food, their turds. I could hear dogs but couldn't see any. Three separate barns stood in the sun, all in pretty bad shape. The smallest had a big triangular hole in the roof.

'Murray around?' I said to the first person I found. She looked a few years older than me, dressed like a scarecrow. She pointed, lifted her chin, went back to sorting through the box at her feet. I made my way behind the barn, treading carefully. From there you could see pretty far up into the Sierras, though I mostly saw smoke.

Over by a stand of dogwood, I found what I took to

be Murray. Jeans, black T-shirt, Cardinals cap, beard with a bit of grey. He was brushing a donkey with what looked like a good deal of tenderness. The donkey, grey and skinny, had its eyes closed and looked happy. Between Murray's lips was a crooked, hand-rolled cigarette that needed relit. He turned to watch me come, still brushing the animal but watching too.

'You must be here to lay the sewer pipes,' he said.

'On my way to work.'

My voice seemed to startle the donkey. Murray patted and shushed it. 'Never seen stilettos, is all,' he said. 'Nor a stylish-looking blouse for that matter. Too bad, huh, girl? Such a sheltered life.'

I told him he had a nice place and asked if he'd be all right with Sean coming by and helping out some with the llamas.

'Calvin and Hobbes? Those two pretty well look after themselves.' He paused to get his smoke going. The veins on his forearms bulged out, I noticed, but more from being skinny than muscular. 'But our mutual friend Prisha told me a little about your kid.'

I felt a little kick. 'Is that right.'

He waved his smoking hand in a way that I assume was meant to reassure me. 'Only that he's having some trouble, y'know—coming back to earth.' He took a drag and blew it out, away from both the donkey and me. 'Jesus, who can blame him? Shit these kids got to wade through over there, beats me how any of them make it back—what's the word—*intact*.'

I was glad for my sunglasses then. 'It might only be

once or twice. Or maybe the llama thing'll wear out and you can put him to work. He's real –'

I meant to say *strong*. But I couldn't get it out. My throat and tongue felt swollen and my eyes stung. Maybe it was the donkey, standing there all loyal and happy, coat all brushed and shiny, ribs showing through. Maybe it was the dust.

My mom always told me, better to have a man fear you than pity you. Which you couldn't say got her very far. But I sucked in a breath and straightened up.

'He's a hard worker,' I croaked. 'No need to cut him any slack.'

Murray took another drag. He had an unhurried vibe that I appreciated. 'Golden Peak, huh?' He nodded at my chest. 'What's that like?'

'Can't beat it for buffet. Other than that, I guess you could say we both work with animals.'

He laughed and the donkey flinched. 'Oh, this here isn't work. Seen plenty of work in my time and being out in the sun with these guys'll beat it every time.'

'Retired?'

He swung his head from side to side. 'I prefer to think of it as proceeding. Proceeding on a different path.'

'Guess I missed the off-ramp for that one.'

He chuckled again and stooped to grind his smoke out on his boot.

'I'll send him over tomorrow,' I said. When he said sure, I thanked him and turned and did my best to walk back to my car over the hard, dry ground in a way that would give him no choice but to look.

'Hey,' he called after me. 'Don't you wanna see 'em?'

I half turned my head, flicked my hair, kept going. 'Don't you?'

The one that did it turned out to have been set. Which wasn't all that unusual, except in this case a firefighter did the setting. Supposedly he needed the overtime and also wanted to prove himself to his new crew. So they said on the news. My feeling was, if you're offering more than one excuse, best keep quiet and take your licks.

They called it the Amagan Fire. Never got big enough to be a complex, but I guess it's not the size so much as where it goes.

On the second day they said it was thirty per cent contained. But then something changed and it was back to ten per cent, five. Moving in unexpected ways, they said, which seemed like a joke, or a line from a song. Word came down from upstairs that an evac plan was in place, but the casino would remain fully operational until the authorities demanded otherwise. *Peakers should remain upbeat, reassuring clients and distracting them from the current situation.* 'Business as usual, then,' Prisha said. Except now the situation was clearly visible from the restaurant.

People sat chewing, licking their fingers, staring out at the smoke and flames like it was a projection on a screen. They asked me about it as if we'd laid it on as entertainment. Was it as close as it looked, was it under control? Closer, I wanted to say, and not even close.

Still, they kept coming, stuffing their faces, going back

for more. Waddling off to blow a few bucks on the slots. And why not? Lose it all tomorrow if the wind swung around. Lose it all even if it didn't.

I was halfway through a shift when I spotted him, Murray, moseying in like a reg. The TVs all had Donald Trump on repeat, announcing he was running for president. It was a week or so since I'd stopped by the ranch. Sean had been over there every day, and now at night instead of watching TV he was watching llama videos for hours at a time on the computer in the hallway. Who knew there were so many? Llamas smiling, llamas falling down, llamas wearing hats or dancing. Sometimes he laughed till he cried, others the reverse. It all seemed like too much llama—I was starting to regret the whole thing. But at least he was out in the sun most days and he'd lost interest in SpongeBob and the rest of that crap.

Murray looked to have thrown on a clean shirt, and his hair was wet and combed, the grey parts darkened by damp. I could picture him, out in the lot, emptying his canteen over his head and finding an old comb on the floor of his truck.

'Guess they're letting in all comers tonight,' I said, once I got a second to stop by his table.

He leaned back and patted his little pot belly, which was round enough for his T-shirt to cling to it. 'Hungry work, brushing donkeys.' I made a face to let him know I wasn't going to let him off that easy. 'Been meaning to make the drive up here for a while, see what the fuss is about.'

'There's a fuss?'

'Your reputation precedes you.'

I poured him some water, though it wasn't my table. 'No girl likes to hear that.'

He laughed. 'Any tips? All these options could overwhelm a man who lives on Bush's Grillin' Beans and a mean egg scramble.'

'Go slow, choose wisely. Can't tell you how many turkeys I've seen make themselves sick trying to eat their way across the room.'

He nodded and there was a little pause. 'So how slow do I need to go to be finishing up around the same time as you?'

'Haven't met a man yet who could manage that.'

He blushed then, bless him. Sipped his water, smiling. I think he was beginning to realize what he was dealing with. I put my hand on his shoulder.

Later we stood by my car, looking out from the parking structure on to the hills. You couldn't see the fire itself, but the smoky clouds were lit orange from beneath. The whole night had an eerie, end-of-days feeling, but I was getting used to that.

'So how's he doing?' I yawned.

Murray lit a smoke, leaning on the waist-high concrete wall. I almost said something about there being plenty of smoke in the air as it was, but it was 2.05 and I'd been being delightful for ten straight hours. 'Hard to tell,' he said.

'He's hanging with the llamas, though?'

'Exclusively. Hasn't said more than a few words to me

or anyone else. But I've heard him on the breeze, y'know. Shooting the shiatzu.'

I turned my head. 'With Calvin and Hobbes?'

'Not unusual. You should hear some of the confessions those poor creatures have to endure. Day-long anecdotes, marital beefs. Cheaper than therapy, I guess.'

'And I thought vocalizing your shit wasn't in the military manual.'

He nodded, blew smoke and ground out the butt. I rummaged in my purse for my keys.

'You get a night off?' Murray said, turning. I told him. 'So you'd be free for dinner next Monday, then?'

'Not impossible,' I said, climbing into the car and lowering the window. He asked for my number and I watched him try to get it into his little flip-phone. 'Need some help there, clumsy-thumbs?'

He handed it over. I'd asked Prisha about him earlier that week, what she knew about that *different path*. She said no one had ever got the whole story out of him, but the rumour was he'd sold a meat-processing plant somewhere in Missouri, split from his wife (kids grown and gone) and up and moved to Placer County when he saw the ranch listed in some horse-trader paper. Processing as in slaughterhouse, I said. Prisha shrugged.

As I drove away, I saw him gazing around, trying, I think, to remember where he'd parked. And maybe it's good that it ended like that. Lost, but only temporarily, with something still to look forward to.

*

Viv seemed jumpy. Arturo from upstairs had spooked her with a look—she was keeping it all off-site for a while. 'Can I come by in the morning? I'll bring Nathan,' she said. We were in the break room, rubbing our feet. 'I know he'd love to meet Sean. Signing up when he turns eighteen, so he says.' I must have made a face because she went on, 'Well, he won't be going to frickin' Stanford, that's for sure. Principal says he prefers fighting to talking things through. I'm like, so we've established he's male.'

When I got home that night and told Sean, he looked like he might put the computer through the window. 'Who the fuck is Arturo?'

'It's just a few more hours, sweetie. You want me to lose my job?'

He grabbed his keys and headed for the door. I stepped in front. When he tried to go around, I moved.

'Get out of my way, Mom.'

I shook my head. 'We made a deal.'

I could smell the sweat and llama on him, like damp wool laced with manure. Muddy smudges on his forehead and cheek. He tried to push past and I pushed back. He tried to shove me sideways and I kneed him in the balls. He went down, doubled over, moaning. I thought he was going to throw up. 'What the *fuck*, Mom.'

Back when he was deployed, he'd often call when I was sleeping. It was partly my schedule, partly the time difference. We'd talk for however long he had, regular stuff, what was he eating, how was the weather, how were his buddies. Afterwards, I'd go back to sleep, and later, when I got up, I'd have to really think whether it had actually happened. Did we talk, for real? Or did I dream it? Did we *communicate* in my sleep? We never talked nicer than on those calls. Or, at least, that's how I remember them.

Now, my voice came out shakier than I wanted, but maybe that was good. 'I swear to Christ I will shoot you in the heart before I let you buy any more of that rat-poison junk from some asshole in a goddamn Safeway parking lot.' I was standing over him, still in my heels, skirt freshly stained from a plate of chicken wings that someone lost control of. 'Viv'll be here in the morning. Until then all you're going to do is take a long shower, clean up your trash and get your sheets out of the dryer so we can pull them back on.'

Eventually he dragged himself up and looked at me, though not in the eye. He called me something no one had called me since his father took off. But when he walked by me it was towards the stairs, not the door. And as I slipped off my shoes and dropped on to the couch, I heard the shower start to run.

At 11.04 the next morning he was limping around the living room, breathing heavy, squirming in his skin. His nose was running like a soda fountain and he kept wiping it on his snot-slick forearm.

'Why you got to have the air so cranked?'

The air wasn't even on, but he was shivering like a puppy in a blizzard. Half an hour earlier he'd been sweating bullets, smashing around the place, closing the blinds to block the sun. His hair was sticking up on one side. It was nearly down to his eyebrows by then, which was nice after all those years of high-and-tights. I wanted to run my fingers through it, like I did when he was little. But he'd probably break my arm before I even made contact.

'You said eleven,' he said, peering through the blinds.

'How're Calvin and Hobbes doing?'

He shook his head like he knew what I was up to and wasn't going to fall for it. But I could tell he wanted to say something kind.

'One more time,' I said.

He grabbed at his hair, went back to pacing and let out a big, almost comical groan. 'I know the drill, Mom.'

'So –'

'I take the kid out back, you get the stuff.'

'And how many words about pills or drugs do you say in front of Nathan?'

'None! Zero! Jesus Christ!'

The doorbell rang. 'Sit your butt down.' I heard my tone—it was the same one I used to use on Joey, back before the vet put him to sleep.

Viv's kid looked older than I expected. I guess it's all the hormones and junk in the milk. She'd told me he was thirteen but he looked more like a college quarterback with adult acne. His T-shirt said 'Odd Future' on it and his shorts went way below his knees.

'Morning, all,' Viv said. 'Had some trouble getting this guy out of bed.'

Sean was in the armchair, skinny, clammy, snotty, bouncing one knee like he was pumping up a tyre. I saw him through their eyes and he looked like shit. Viv and Nathan hovered nervously. I guess they'd been expecting more of your all-American hero—the kind of veteran you see getting medals pinned on their puffed-out chest at some fancy White House shindig.

'Your mom tells me you want to serve when you graduate,' I said to Nathan.

'Damn straight,' he said, but there was no conviction.

'Sean,' I said, 'why don't you grab Nathan a soda and show him out back?' I turned back to Nathan. 'Sean's got a pretty cool rope swing back there. Had it since he was your age, more or less.'

The kid made a face like, *How old d'you think I am?* But Sean got up and hustled him into the kitchen. 'Let's go,' he said. Eyes on the prize.

'Cute kid,' I said to Viv once the back door swung shut.

'Moody little bastard is what he is.' She was digging for the pills in her purse.

'Looks healthy, at least.' I handed her the cash and slipped the baggy into the front pocket of my hoodie.

'They helping the pain some?'

I shrugged, shook my head. 'Doc says that hip's gonna hurt long term.'

'Hear about the fire?' she said, glancing behind me a little nervously, trying to see out to the yard. I was about to say it was fine if she wanted to grab her boy and go. But before I could, a godawful scream started up back there and we both rushed through the kitchen and out the door.

The two boys were tangled in the dirt. Sean had Nathan in some kind of chokehold, and he wasn't fooling around.

Nathan was silent, his face turning purple, tears coming down his cheeks. The neighbour's mutts were barking madly at the fence.

'Whoa there, Seany.' I edged towards him, arms out. 'Let's relax now, okay?'

That made him growl and yank even harder on Nathan's arm. It was twisted so far behind I thought for sure we'd hear it snap.

My heart was thumping. 'C'mon, sweetie, let him go. Let him go and come inside. I've got your pills, okay? Come take a pill and relax.'

'Let him go, you fucking psycho!' That was Viv, stepping forward, looking around for something to swing at his head. Before she found anything, Sean eased up and pushed Nathan down on to the dirt.

'You watch your mouth, you little shit-for-brains,' he said, pointing with a shaking finger. 'You don't know a goddamn thing.'

Nathan scrambled up and over to his mom, then crouched behind her, gasping and sobbing.

'What the hell could he say to deserve that?' Viv said, putting an arm around her son. 'He's a kid, for Christ's sake.'

'I just asked him if it's true what I heard,' Nathan said, half whining, half cocky.

Uh oh, I thought.

'What the hell did you hear?' Viv said.

'That he left –' He sniffled. 'That he left his buddies who got hurt. Ran away and got shot right in the ass.'

Sean stepped forward and I got between them. 'Don't

make me knee you in the balls again, bud.' I turned to Viv and gave her a look.

'Oh, don't worry, we're leaving.' I had a feeling she wished she could call the cops. 'Let's go, baby,' she said, leading hunched Nathan back around the side of the house. 'You're fine.'

'Sorry, Viv, really,' I called after them.

As soon as her truck fired up and pulled away, Sean held out his hands, two cupped palms together.

Once he'd calmed down and headed out, I took a long shower and shaved my legs, which I've always done when I need to feel better, even if it's only been a day. I made coffee, fried bacon and generally tried to act like a regular person eating Saturday brunch. But anyone who works nights will tell you your free time before a shift never really feels free. It's like a megaphone countdown at the back of your mind.

I was sitting down to eat when the phone rang. I almost let it go. Who calls a landline these days, anyhow? But when your kid's in the military, you always pick up.

It was Tory. 'Is he there?'

I told her he was not. 'What's going on, sweetie?' I was gazing at my bacon, wishing I'd brought my plate over to the counter.

'He needs to stop, all right? Stop with the emails. Stop with the freaking llama videos.'

'He's sending you those?'

'Like ten a night! And not even ten links in one email—ten *separate* emails.'

I felt my shoulders sag. 'I didn't know.'

'What is he, schizo now? Because this is the weirdest shit he's pulled by far.'

'He's . . .' I had no idea what to say. 'We're working it out. I guess he said there was a llama in some movie you always liked and –'

'*Napoleon Dynamite*? I hate that stupid movie! *He's* the one that always wanted to watch it.'

I thought about that for a second. 'He's been spending time at this –'

'I don't actually care, though, y'know? Not my problem. I've got a colicky baby to deal with and a boyfriend who wants to know why my phone's blowing up all night long.'

I hadn't even heard she was pregnant. It was longer than I thought since I'd seen her. 'Can't you put it on silent? Or mark him as junk?'

I heard a baby wailing as she hung up. The bacon was still warm but didn't taste as good as I needed it to.

Since Sean started at the ranch, I'd been enjoying the peace around here. To have the TV sitting there, cartoon-free and silent, was a relief. But after I'd eaten and washed up and picked up after him—I found a lonesome Peep peeking out between two throw pillows, head still intact—the quiet started to bother me. Which is why I switched on the radio, which is how I finally heard.

You'd need a weathergirl or firefighter to explain it, especially now some time has passed. But the wind had shifted overnight and the fire had hurried up out of the valley, up to the ridge from where I guess it got a pretty nice view of the dried-up lake to the west and decided it wanted to head in that direction at what the radio described as 'an alarming rate'. The Peak was evacuating, though the fire wasn't showing much interest in the place. But properties to the north were looking less safe, and people were being told to move, even the ones with defensible space, even the ones too old and frail to take out their own trashcans on a Thursday night, let alone throw their whole entire lives into a car and drive off into the smoky sunset.

I guess that mention of the casino threw me off, because it was only after I switched on the TV and saw the smoke from the helicopter cameras and the flames tearing down the hills like lava pouring out of a volcano—only then did I think of the ranch. The ranch, and Murray. And Sean.

Neither picked up. I tried again as I backed one-handed out of the driveway and gunned down Donner, blazing through stop signs, calling the two of them alternately, yelling for someone to pick the hell up, pick the hell up, you sons of bitches. When I turned on to Voorhies it was suddenly there, this monster column of white-grey smoke, towering like a monument.

I took the back roads in case the freeway was bad. I must've been doing eighty or ninety—some of those corners nearly had me flipping. I saw a few pickups loaded high with black trash bags and furniture, bird cages and picture frames, old wooden cribs and floor lamps, all headed in the other direction, waving at me with their eyes wide. From a distance, the smoke had seemed high and remote, but as I got closer it got thicker and lower. Even with the A/C blasting I could feel that raw, ferocious heat.

I turned on to Green Valley Road, coughing. Through the drifting smoke I saw the roadblock up ahead. Fire trucks, cop cars, ambulances, the KCRA 3 van with its dish on top. I ditched the car close to all the others, thinking maybe I would start walking. That was when I noticed I was barefoot. Besides, I was barely out of the car when a CHP came over and asked if everything was all right.

'You tell me,' I said. He was young and professional-looking, shoulders pulled back. When he looked right at me, I could see myself in his sunglasses. The blacktop was scorching the soles of my feet.

'Can't let you go any farther, ma'am. Fire's moving pretty good now and we've got a situation on a property a little ways up.'

'You mean the ranch? Murray's ranch?'

He repositioned himself. 'You have some connection to the property?'

'What do you mean a situation? You're getting everybody out, right?'

He turned away, looking beyond all the vehicles towards the fire. Everything was thick with heat, like the air itself was melting. I could see a tree burning, blackened skeletons of its brothers behind, still-green untouched ones in front. You could almost hear them scream.

'Murray's my fiancé,' I said. It just came out. 'And I

think my kid'—I had to cough again—'I think my kid's over there too.'

He turned back to me. 'Your son?'

Yes, I told him, my son, Sean. 'Why? What's going on?'

Wait here. That was all he said. I watched him conferring with a couple cops. All three of them looked over at me and went back to their huddle. A very bad feeling was building up. I went to get my phone from inside the car and found it vibrating on the passenger seat. My phone didn't know the number but I knew who it would be.

'I can't get any closer,' I said.

'Gloria?' He was shouting, frantic, out of breath. 'Gloria, are you there?'

'Is he with you? Are you guys all right?'

'He wouldn't come! Kid would not come. We had to save the healthiest, the youngest, y'know? The younger horses, the dogs. There was no time, it came down so fast. Of course I'd save them all, but there wasn't time, I had to make decisions, just make them and act, right? I had to *act*.'

'Slow down, slow—what do you mean, he wouldn't come?'

'He had a fucking *pistol*, Gloria. I was begging and begging but he wouldn't listen. Just kept pointing it at me and yanking on those ropes. I mean those llamas were flipping out, they wanted to turn and run but there was nowhere left to go. And I *told* him, *we can't save them, we can't save them, we have to go NOW, let's go, let's go!* But he wouldn't come. *I won't leave them, I won't fucking leave them . . .*'

He kept talking, but I didn't hear it. I dropped the phone on to the passenger seat. All the heat was draining out of me, I was freezing in the middle of a fire. It felt like my blood was being replaced, switched out with some other toxic substance, headed straight for my brain, straight for my heart.

Two more news vans were pulling up. FOX40, ABC10. A cop, not the chipper but one of the others, was walking towards me, hands on belt. He took off his glasses to look at me but all I saw was smoke.

11. Antediluvian

The younger man had been lingering for a while near the bar when a timid waitress asked Pointer if he might be willing to share his table. The two shook hands, Ned—that was the young man's name—apologizing as if he had let a door swing shut in Pointer's face.

'Please,' Pointer said, lifting his chin to indicate the other diners, European couples, holding hands across the tables, sharing bottles of chilled white wine they would finish off back in their rooms. 'I'm the old sod spoiling the mood.'

Ned said he lived in Nairobi, where he taught English to business students. Before that, he'd been an estate agent in Clapham Junction—not a very good one. His hair was jaw-length, unwashed and uncombed, and he had a way of talking down and to the side as if unsure he had anything of value to offer.

'Mostly a girl,' he said, when Pointer asked what, apart from the obvious, had inspired the big move. 'Unless that's the obvious.' Pointer kept his own hair neat, always had, even during long stints in the field. He detected a story Ned wasn't eager to share, and he frankly wasn't desperate to hear.

Hotel Dahoma, sealed off by automated gates and high walls topped with barbed wire, was built into the heart of an old fishing village on the north-east coast of Unguja, the largest island in the archipelago. It had seen a spate of robberies the previous year, culminating in the murder-by-stabbing of a Dane who'd stumbled upon two thieves at work in his room, and off-season rates had halved.

'No way I could afford it otherwise,' said Ned.

Pointer agreed, though in truth he was in the financial shape of his life. A recent flurry of interest had inspired new editions of two of his books, and a retrospective at the RGS. At his sons' insistence, he had booked this trip to Zanzibar—somewhere, for all his travels, he had never reached—as a sort of reward. Richie and James, both up in London with wives and kids, had expressed concern about him moping around the Somerset cottage. He had always been an absent, active father, disappearing at a day's notice to cover a nascent coup against Amin or to dash in a Press vest down Ledra Street, reloading his Nikon F while, beside him, a Cypriot soldier plugged with two fingers a hole in his own throat. Though he was pushing seventy-four, it troubled his sons to see him languish in a routine of crosswords, gardening and lengths of the local pool.

'Wasn't too keen at first,' he told Ned. 'Swanky hotels were never really me.' He'd grown up in the Finsbury Park tenements—in a two-room flat with shared outhouse and neighbours upstairs smashing milk bottles in the sink so as not to have to lug them down to the doorstep—and had always been more comfortable camping rough than lounging in five-star luxury. But getting something pricey at a bargain rate was irresistible. Like Ned, and probably everyone else, he wouldn't have picked the Dahoma were it not for that Dane's bad luck. But while the thought of what happened that night last year didn't trouble Pointer, he sensed, as they talked, that for Ned it cast a kind of shadow. More than one guest, turning in after dinner, would be knocking loudly before unlocking their doors.

Electric light lapped at the top of the beach. Waiters in creased, ill-fitting white shirts hurried to relight lanterns blown out by the onshore wind. A new couple entered the restaurant. The woman looked to be in her late twenties, long dark hair, strong jaw, big alluring eyes, slovenly posture contrasting with a fine purple cocktail dress. The man, who had black hair styled like a little fin, seemed younger, though perhaps it was only that he hadn't dressed up.

'Hundred quid says they're Londoners,' Pointer said.

As the two men ate their pineapple and ice cream, the woman mounted a barstool somewhat clumsily, crossing her long, pale legs. Pointer succumbed to a vision in which she led him by the hand on to the dark beach, beyond the lights but still close enough to hear the murmur of voices, arranged him deftly on his back on the sand, stepped out of her knickers, lifted her dress. Afterwards, she would leave him sprawled, return to the bar for another cocktail.

'I suppose they want our table,' Ned said. Pointer nodded and they finished their desserts.

*

The tide was out for much of the day, leaving a shallow lagoon protected by a reef. *Mashua* plied the deeper water beyond, and across the horizon slunk cargo ships heading north to the Gulf or south to the Cape.

On the second afternoon, while the couples lay out around the pool, Pointer walked the beach. It was nice to watch the tiny white crabs dash back to their holes as he approached. Beyond the hotels lay the low shacks of the village. Fishermen, children, women wrapped loosely in yellow-and-orange cloth, seemed surprised at first to see him out there. By the third day, he had become unremarkable. On the fourth, Ned joined him on his long stroll, and a mile or two from the hotel they came upon a group of boys chasing a deflated plastic football. The two men were quickly absorbed into the game, Pointer accepting a position in goal, lumbering between his posts—clumps of dry wrack—as best he could. Diving was out of the question, but the boys cheered whether or not he made a save. They especially loved Ned, who had a mean Cruyff Turn in his repertoire, and argued fiercely about which team he would join.

'You've got a little fan club there,' Pointer said as they made their way back, sore-footed and sweaty. Ned only smiled, shook his head.

That evening, the London girl came into the restaurant alone, carrying a paperback, barefoot this time in a navy vest and denim shorts. The waiter cleared her husband's place. Without hesitation, Pointer rose and went over, returning with her cutlery, napkin and glass, the woman following behind.

Nicola lived in Battersea with her fiancé, or rather, husband—'Haven't quite got the hang of that yet'—who had gone down with food poisoning overnight. His name was Suve. 'He thinks it was the crab salad.'

'We had that,' said Pointer, 'didn't we, Ned? We're both right as rain.' He thumped himself twice in the gut.

'You must be made of sterner stuff,' Nicola said, smiling.

'You've married the wrong man,' Pointer said, winking at Ned.

Up close and dressed down, she was less imposing, with narrow shoulders and small teeth, younger than she had seemed that first night. She was a barrister, she told them—long hours, but she loved it. As if under cross-examination, she confessed to a sheltered childhood, Home Counties suburban, the younger of two girls. Her sister, Melissa—eight months pregnant with a child conceived, as far as anyone could tell, during a holiday fling with an anonymous Frenchman—had apparently wept at such volume during the exchange of vows that the reverend had had to repeat himself several times, as if he were the one nervously pledging. Suve's family, meanwhile, had refused to attend, protesting his decision to marry a white girl in a church rather than wait for a match to be arranged.

'Good lad,' Pointer said.

They wanted to talk about his work—people always did. But beyond specific anecdotes, it was hard to know what to say. He had travelled to places most Brits avoided, lived from one assignment to the next, been serially unfaithful to one wife and then another, missed most of the significant moments in his children's lives, spent too many nights in squalid little rooms, sniper fire streaking past the windows. People wanted him to be haunted, for his eyes to fill with tears at some memory or other—that Cambodian woman he'd photographed, say, cradling her sister's bloated corpse. They wanted guilt, trauma, desolation, but he had never suffered like that. His work was an addiction he'd been glad to feed— what else was there to say?

Nicola and Ned seemed pleased to realize they knew the picture that had brought his name back into the lights. It had made the front pages the previous summer, including the international editions Ned picked up. Nicola asked how it came about.

When the trouble started, Pointer told them, he was staying with James and his wife in East Dulwich, mostly watching cricket on TV. The live footage of the riots had awakened something in him, and from the moment he emerged, camera in hand, out of the Tube at Bethnal Green into a chaos of burning cars and broken glass and shrieking sirens, he'd enjoyed himself immensely. He followed the skirmishes as they spilled from street to street, camera pressed to his face. More than one hooded looter howled at him, threatened to smash his camera. He was unfazed. That evening, on James's laptop, he studied the shots. One stood out immediately—a white man in his early thirties, apparently wearing plaid pyjamas, no mask or scarf to shield his face, punching an Asian policeman in the mouth as another officer, a Black woman, struggled to restrain him.

Send it in, James had said. There were fifty more filming on their phones, Pointer told him. But his reluctance sounded hollow even to him. Later that year the picture won a couple of awards, and Pointer had to get his good suit dry-cleaned.

'We were in Brighton that weekend, thank God,' Nicola said. She'd almost bought one of his books for her uncle last Christmas.

'Almost?' Pointer said.

Emptying the last of the wine into their glasses, she mentioned that she and Suve were booked to snorkel in the morning. No way would he be up to it, she said, and she didn't fancy going alone. Pointer saw at once that the younger man was keen. 'I'm game if Ned is,' he said.

That night, he dreamed about the boys on the beach, kicking their ball around. The sunlight fell on them in waves, laughter on the breeze, lagoon behind them smooth and blue. Then, one by one, they turned on him, glaring, each suddenly a replica of an Eritrean child he had photographed during the '85 famine—skeletal, bulbous-bellied, glint of accusation in the dying eyes—a memory that had surfaced now and then over the years but never so threateningly. Now the duplicates of that doomed boy dragged their wasted forms towards him, arms extended in supplication, until something shifted and the beach disappeared, and as he lay on his bed they tapped on the glass with crooked, bony fingers, unblinking, begging to come inside.

The dive centre was half a mile to the north. The three of them walked along the beach, chewing warm bread rolls from the buffet, sun emerging out of the ocean, tinting the sand pink. Pointer detected a new ease between Ned and Nicola. 'Late night for you youngsters, was it?'

'Someone decided Sambucas were a good idea,' Ned said.

'I'm honeymooning,' Nicola said, 'and my husband's got the shits. What's a girl supposed to do?'

Beyond the lagoon, the boat rolled with the swell. While the divers checked tanks and scrutinized gauges, Nicola threw up off the side. For twenty minutes they sailed over deep, dark water—a chalkboard back at the centre had boasted four shark sightings in the last week—until the water paled and cleared over an off-shore reef. They were close to uninhabited Mnemba, Unguja little more than a distant green layer. With a yelp, Nicola dropped into the water, adjusting her mask with the help of Alhaadi, their guide. Pointer followed and was greeted by a vision—hundreds of fish of every colour and size swimming through the coral crags—so startling he almost neglected to blow out his snorkel. The three of them swam behind Alhaadi, lost in their marvelling, eyes caught by one fluorescent burst of movement after another. Sunlight filtered down through the clear water, casting their shadows on the reef.

Pointer began to detect some trace of nearby panic. He saw Nicola swimming scrappily away, kicking and flailing, notes of distress sounding through the chamber of her snorkel. Ned had stopped too. Alhaadi dived again. Pointer signalled to him. Nicola was swimming for the boat, thirty metres away, her mask discarded, floating behind.

'I've been stung!' she cried.

By the time they were all on deck, the other divers still off somewhere trawling the depths, welts had appeared on her calf. The imprint of trailing tentacles was clear, red and raw like a chemical burn. She winced and whimpered as Alhaadi doused it with hot water.

'Was it a jellyfish?' asked Ned.

She didn't know, she hadn't seen. Hunching over, she began to shiver. The pain was getting worse, she said, and spreading. 'Spreading where?' Pointer said. With a shaking hand she indicated her kidneys, her spine. Soon she couldn't hold herself up, head lolling helplessly.

'She needs air!' Ned shouted, grabbing an oxygen tank from the scuba gear and pushing the mouthpiece between her bluing lips.

Pointer pulled Alhaadi aside. 'What does she need?'

The guide watched Nicola without urgency. Ned's arms were clasped around her, holding her up, his expression full of dread. 'Maybe cortisone?' Alhaadi shrugged.

'Is it on the boat?'

'What's he saying?' Ned yelled.

Pointer repeated Alhaadi's guess.

'He *thinks*? Does anybody *know*?' He looked frantically at Nicola and back at the guide. 'For Christ's sake, she's—don't just stand there like—get on the radio! Call a fucking doctor!'

Alhaadi whistled impassively across the glinting water to another man in a small RIB trailing the divers. Soon

Pointer and Ned were lifting Nicola, by now grimly pale, barely conscious, shaking, down into the RIB. Alhaadi passed them the tank—he couldn't leave the boat.

Careening towards shore, outboard howling, Pointer felt more exhilarated than he had since that day in Bethnal Green. He watched Ned cradling Nicola, stroking her hair and talking in her ear. The younger man's face was ashen. Pointer thought of their conversation on the first night. There was, he saw, more than one woman in Ned's arms, more than one life at stake.

The tide was dropping fast as they neared the lagoon. Pointer and Ned carried Nicola's limp form up the beach into the dive centre, laying her out on a bench, covering her with dry towels. The doctor, called by the woman on duty, was supposedly hurrying up the coast from Mwambe. Fifteen minutes, the woman said. Pointer lasted only five before he had to step outside. Nicola's condition was troubling, but it was Ned's anguish that finally became unbearable. The desperation in the young man's eyes, the devotion to this woman little more than a stranger and a newlywed at that, struck him as by far the more fatal affliction.

The doctor, a jovial, bearded Belgian with wire-rimmed glasses, helped her out of her wetsuit and administered the hydrocortisone. It was probably a man o' war, he explained—not strictly a jellyfish. As the pain eased, colour returned to her face. Soon she was talking, thanking the doctor, shaking her head. Pointer watched Ned recovering too, straightening and moving away from the bench, seeming to gather himself.

'Ned, why don't you jog on down the beach and fetch Nicola's chappie.'

'Oh, thanks, Ned,' she said dreamily. She was sitting up in her black-and-red swimsuit, white smear of ointment on her wound. 'Tell him not to worry, though, would you? Tell him I'm not dying or anything.'

Ned's head hung for a moment before he nodded.

Pointer dined alone that night, his last at the Dahoma. No sign of the others. The waiting staff broke into song, swaying in a line with their hands held up, smiling for the clapping guests.

The dream came again. He exploded into wakefulness, groping for the lamp. In his head, he listed men who had wound up caving. Some he had called friends. Hazlett, Constantini. Even Berman. For years, he'd pitied them—pansies the lot. Not up to the job, doomed from the start by an in-built weakness, a fatal flaw like a crack through a plate—the work just widened the fissure. But now he sensed them gathering around him in the dark, arms linked in support.

Sunrise found him swimming the lagoon. With open eyes he pushed down to the bottom, grabbing fistfuls of sand, watching it disperse. The light was dim but gilded. When he surfaced and saw the sky filling with colour, he felt all the days behind him, strewn like spent canisters of film. Later, he walked south on the beach, hoping to find the football boys, but that stretch of sand was bare, marked only by a collage of footprints and the clumps of dry seaweed that had been his posts. He walked on, into the wilder expanses beyond the village, monkeys moving and screeching in the branches, their long, tentacular tails never still. Up ahead, he saw a figure sitting on a hunk of driftwood. He raised an arm and Ned, in yellow shorts and a tatty short-sleeved shirt, hair blowing into his eyes, did the same.

'Beat me to it,' Pointer said.

The younger man shifted, patting the bone-smooth wood, and the two of them sat side by side in silence, regarding the lagoon and the surf beyond. Gulls hung in the breeze and from their sandy catacombs the little crabs began to re-emerge.

'What was her name?' Pointer said at last.

Ned shook his head. 'I made a fool of myself.'

Pointer waved that away. 'If you hadn't, I would have.'

Standing and stepping two paces forward, the younger man made marks in the sand with his toe. 'Penny,' he said eventually. 'She was killed on the road between Nairobi and Garissa, riding on top of a bus that went into a ditch. It made all the papers back home, though I missed it at first. Someone said they saw her passing through the air. Isn't that perfect?'

'Where were you?'

'In London. She'd been away a few years by then, but I'd convinced myself she'd be back any day.'

Pointer nodded, pushed his thin grey hair back off his forehead. 'I was in Chad once, out in the desert. I've never been one for mysticism, but there's something about the desert when you're really out there in it. The guide showed us how to slide down the dunes on our bare feet—the sand was so smooth and tightly packed, it was like skidding down a wet pane of glass. Sang like a glass too. You wet your finger and trace around the rim, you know? That beautiful note. It was like that. Kept at it for hours, we did, till our feet were in ruins. Sang and sang, those dunes.'

Ned turned to look back at him, his expression impossible to see with the sun so bright behind.

'Passing through the air,' Pointer said.

He was packing when Nicola knocked on his door. She wore no make-up, hair tied back. Suve was at the dive centre giving them hell. She was supposed to be resting. 'But I didn't want to miss you before you left.'

He asked her how she was feeling. Much better, she said, though the sting still burned. Had she been to see Ned?

'Not yet. But I will.' She looked at his half-packed suitcase. 'Bet you'll be glad to get home.'

He shook his head. One night in Stone Town and then back to the empty Somerset cottage, back to the garden and Radio 4 and those endless unfinished crosswords. And that was only a prelude to the real shit—wasting away in some sterile dump, surrounded by other infirm old buggers, the air rank with piss and soup, nurses lifting him on to the toilet, wiping him when he was done. No—better to be dead.

She leaned forward to say goodbye, arms clasped lightly around him. He pressed her body into his, feeling her breasts against his ribs, one hand above her buttocks, one between her shoulder blades. Breathing in the smell of her, he kissed her throat like a schoolboy trying to leave a mark.

'Bill,' she said calmly. 'Bill, come on now.'

She let her arms drop, but that was it. The lack of resistance was awful. He squeezed harder, stunned by the weakness of his arms—back in the day, he could've snapped such a skinny thing in two. She was waiting for him to let go, and finally he did, his head bowed.

'Forgive me,' he said. 'I –'

'No harm done,' she said. 'But I'm a married woman these days. Time to start behaving myself.'

It was the most generous thing she could have said. He felt a flood of gratitude, so different from the hunger of a moment before. His throat was full and he had to swallow before he could speak. 'He's a lucky man,' he said.

She winked, and lowered her voice to a whisper. 'You have no idea.'

His driver, Philip, a serious man with prominent ears, declared himself an Arsenal fan, indicating the red-and-white paraphernalia scattered across the dashboard.

'Good lad,' Pointer said. 'If you ever make it to a home game, I'll show you my old stomping grounds.' He shifted forward. 'Tell me, the Danish chap killed last year, did you meet him?'

Philip shook his head solemnly. 'No, sir. But his wife, yes. They are honeymoons, you know? I am driving her to Stone Town after, to the consulate.'

'She must've been in rough shape.'

'She did not speak, sir. Her eyes . . .' He shook his head again.

'And they caught the lads involved?'

'Oh, yes, sir. Very easy, same day. It is over, this problem. No more trouble.'

Pointer sat back in his seat, trying to imagine the young widow riding in this car. He could picture her only as Nicola. If it had happened to her—had Suve been the one killed—would she still have managed to speak with Philip as he drove? Yes. He was certain of it.

Suddenly, he was epically tired. Lush, ragged sugarcane fields blurred past. He watched them and, after a while, slept.

He was jarred awake by tapping on the tinted glass. They had stopped somewhere in the tattered interior amid low and half-built houses. A thunderous rain was coming down—it seemed another country. Drenched people surrounded the car, peering inside, knocking, men in torn T-shirts, women with infants strapped to their bodies, calling to him in a way he couldn't fathom. Was he dreaming again?

'They are wanting free taxi, sir.' Philip pointed at the bus ahead of them, a pick-up truck with a tarp stretched over the bed and passengers crammed on to narrow benches, spilling over the edge. 'The bus is full and it is raining very strong.'

'They want a lift?'

'Yes, sir. Every day they are knocking, knocking-knocking-knocking.' Philip shrugged. 'Client is paying for nice ride, people are wanting ride for free.'

Pointer looked around at the vacant seats. There were six, seven if he moved his bag, plus another two up front. With the babies they could squeeze in a dozen. The voices grew louder, the car lurching as the hands all pushed and pulled. Through the tinted glass, the wide, white eyes stared, asking a question he'd been trying not to hear for as long as he could remember.

'Well,' he said, 'shall we let them in?'

Acknowledgements

Some elements of Bill Pointer's life and career are based on details recounted by Don McCullin in his book *Unreasonable Behaviour*. Pointer's words, thoughts and actions are fictional.

Some chapters were previously published, in slightly different form: 'Antediluvian' in *Harvard Review* and *The Best Short Stories 2021: The O. Henry Prize Winners*; 'Brazil and Back' in the *Carolina Quarterly*; 'Exactly What You Mean' in *Dig-Boston*; 'Fear the Greeks' in *Lighthouse*; 'Preparation for Trial' in the *White Review* (online); 'Queen of the Forest' in *The Bridport Prize Anthology 2017*; 'The Charges' in *Story*; 'The Hosepipe Ban' at untitledbooks.com; and 'You Must, You Will' in *Granta*. Thank you to the editors and judges involved.

I'm grateful to the Bread Loaf Writers' Conference, the Community of Writers, the Department of English at the UC, Davis, the Elizabeth George Foundation and Writing by Writers. I'm also indebted to all the writers and teachers whose feedback proved crucial.

Thank you to Anthony Byrt, Lucy Corin, Lynn Freed, Pam Houston, Yiyun Li, David Matless, Donna Poppy, Anna Power, Alex Russell and Naomi Williams. Thank you to Max Porter. Thank you to Anna Webber and Seren Adams. Thank you to Mary Mount, Karishma Jobanputra and the Viking team. Thank you to my mother and father. Thank you to my sister, Tessa.

Thank you, Hadley and Elana. Thank you, Jenna.